A Love That's Worth the Risk

Men of Valor
Book Three

By Laura Landon

ARE YOU SIGNED UP FOR DRAGONBLADE'S BLOG?

You'll get the latest news and information on exclusive giveaways, exclusive excerpts, coming releases, sales, free books, cover reveals and more.

Check out our complete list of authors, too!

No spam, no junk. That's a promise!

Sign Up Here

www.dragonbladepublishing.com

Dearest Reader;

Thank you for your support of a small press. At Dragonblade Publishing, we strive to bring you the highest quality Historical Romance from some of the best authors in the business. Without your support, there is no 'us', so we sincerely hope you adore these stories and find some new favorite authors along the way.

Happy Reading!

CEO, Dragonblade Publishing

Additional Dragonblade books by Author Laura Landon

Men of Valor Series
A Love For All Time (Book 1)
A Love That Knows No Bounds (Book 2)
A Love That's Worth The Risk (Book 3)

PROLOGUE

Annalise Washburn stood on the top of the cliff and stared down at the swirling sea below her. The full moon cast ripples of light on the dark water, almost like an invitation. She pulled down the hood of her green velvet cloak to let the cool breeze caress her flushed face. Her heart pounded in her chest and her throat felt tight and raw.

She just wanted this nightmare to end.

As she reached up one hand to brush back a blonde curl, the moonlight reflected on her gold wedding ring. "Jack," she whispered, tears blinding her as she whirled around, ready to run home to him.

But she knew there was nowhere to run. Her husband couldn't save her. Taking a deep breath, Annalise reminded herself that she was out of options. There was only one way to end this nightmare.

Ruthlessly wiping away her tears, she moved toward the small stone bench where Jack had proposed to her. She took off her cloak first, neatly placing it on top of the bench. Then she removed the combs and pins from her hair until the long golden tresses hung loose around her narrow shoulders. Annalise closed her eyes for a moment, then twisted the wedding ring off her finger and gently laid it in the velvet folds of her cloak.

The wind suddenly picked up, blowing her hair wildly around

her and biting through the thin fabric of the simple gray gown she wore. It dried the tears on her face as she cast one last look in the direction of the home she shared with Jack. Annalise could just barely make out the large stone structure in the distance. It all seemed so far away.

"Forgive me," she whispered. Then she walked to the edge of the cliff.

⚜

CHAPTER ONE

MAJOR JACK WASHBURN entered The Angel's Wings Jam and Jelly Shop and walked to where Mrs. Mildred Parker, the manager, stood behind the counter arranging a new display.

"Good morning, gorgeous," Jack greeted her, giving the middle aged manager a heart-stopping smile.

"Good morning, Major," she answered, matching his smile.

"I heard that, Major," Milly's husband said from the back room. "I'll warn you to stop flirting with my wife," he teased.

"You leave the major alone, Anthony. At least he knows how to make a lady feel noticed."

"Are you saying that I don't?" Tony Parker asked as he emerged from the back room.

Milly rounded the counter and walked toward her husband. "You forgot all the pretty words you ever knew after I gave you our firstborn."

"Oh, sweeting," Tony said, coming in close to his wife.

"You behave yourself, Tony." She wagged a finger at him. "We got young lasses working in the store. Miss Livie will give you a piece of her mind if she hears what you say in front of these young ears."

"I didn't say anything, did I, lasses?" he said, turning toward the three young shop girls who stood together near the store window. "It was the major who started this conversation."

"Me?" Jack said, feigning innocence. "I would never start something so inappropriate."

The three girls from the orphanage that Livie had brought in to work in the shop giggled behind their hands.

He winked at them just to see them blush.

"You girls look lively," Milly scolded. "Jenny, unlock the door and put the open sign in the window. It's time to start the day."

Jenny did as she was told, and soon after the door opened, their first customers entered the shop.

Jack stepped to the back room and poured himself a cup of coffee from the pot Milly kept on the cast iron range top. His head hurt like bloody hell again this morning.

"Another late night, Major?" Milly said, following him to the back room. "When are you going to start taking better care of yourself?"

"I take perfect care of myself, Milly. I spread my happiness and pleasing personality around to every pretty female I meet. And even some who are not so pretty."

Jack took a gulp of his coffee that burned his tongue, then gave Milly's cheek a pinch.

"Stop that, you flirt!" she reprimanded him, but he saw the smile on her face. "Don't you think it's time you quit your wild carousing, found yourself a wife, and settled down?"

"Didn't you know, Milly? I've already tried that, and it cured me from ever trying it again." He took another swallow of his coffee, then refilled his cup. When it was full, he ventured a gaze into Milly's face and saw her look of shock and sadness. And pity.

"You were married?" She gasped. "Oh, Major. What happened?"

Bloody hell. What had made him say that? Only his two closest friends and fellow soldiers knew about his disastrous marriage. And he intended to keep it that way. The last thing he wanted was for anyone to find out that Annalise had chosen death over spending her life with him.

Jack envisioned his wife, Annalise, and how deeply they'd

loved each other. How desperately in love they'd been. She'd been the most beautiful woman he'd ever seen, with a laugh that brightened a room and a smile that outshone the sun. He'd never discovered what happened that had forced her to take her life while he was away on an assignment for the Crown, but something tragic must have taken place for someone as vibrant and full of life as his Annie to step off that cliff and into the sea.

If only he'd recovered her body. Then he could have buried her properly. But she had never been found. Jack had to be content knowing she was no doubt buried at the bottom of the sea.

He closed his eyes and heard Milly behind him.

"Are you sure you don't want to talk about it, Major?"

"No, Milly. It's not a story I relish repeating."

She studied his face. "Something tells me it's a story you need to repeat to someone. A man can only drown his troubles for so long before they start to eat him up inside."

"Well, Milly. Don't worry. If I ever need to get my sorry past out in the open, you'll be the first person I come to."

She shook her head, chuckling. "Like I believe that will ever happen."

"Major?" Tony approached him, holding up a folded piece of paper. "This just came for you."

Jack swallowed the last of his coffee, then gave Milly a light kiss on the cheek. "Got to go, Milly," he said, taking the note from Tony. "I've been saved by the call of duty."

"Yes, Major. You go on," she said wryly. "Someone has to save us innocent citizens from all those villains out there."

"That's my sworn duty," Jack bantered.

"I feel safer just knowing you're out there protecting us," she said, then cackled again.

Jack gave her a royal salute, then left the jelly shop and walked toward Commander Waterford's office. Maybe there would be an assignment for Jack, and he'd be gone long enough that Milly would forget what he'd told her, but he doubted it. She was like a dog with a bone. Once she latched on to something, she refused to let it go. And his reference to his marriage was too tasty a bone to let go of. He was afraid Milly would always remember where that bone was buried.

He walked the several blocks to the command post, and stepped inside.

"The commander is waiting for you, Major," a young man in full uniform told him. "You can go right in."

"Are you new, Corporal?" Jack said to the young recruit sitting behind the desk.

"Yes, sir," the corporal said, getting to his feet and greeting Jack with a salute. "Corporal Newquist, sir."

"Well, Corporal, it's good to meet you."

"Yes, sir, Major. Commander Waterford is waiting for you."

"Thank you, Corporal."

Jack knocked twice on Commander Waterford's door and walked in. "Good morning, sir."

Waterford lifted his gaze. "Good morning, Washburn. You look like hell. Rough night?"

Jack straightened his clothes and ran his fingers through his hair. "Yes, sir. It was a short night. Did you need to see me?"

"Yes. Take a seat."

Jack poured himself a cup of coffee and sat in the chair before the commander's desk.

"We have a *matter* that's come to our attention that I'd like you to look into."

"A *matter*?"

"Yes. Smuggling. Illegal contraband."

"Could you be more specific, sir?"

"Opium."

Jack took a swallow of his coffee and winced. It wasn't nearly as good as the coffee Milly made. It was much stronger. And that was what Jack needed this morning. "What do you know about this smuggling ring?"

"Not enough, I'm sorry to say." Waterford sighed. "They're

working out of Whitstable, all over Kent. The leader of the gang has kept himself hidden so far. All we know about the gang members is that they are well organized and professional. They've already killed two of our finest agents, and their deaths weren't quick or humane." He sucked in a deep breath. "Their mutilated bodies were returned to us as a message to leave the smugglers alone, or the same would happen to the next agent we sent."

"I see," Jack said, before finishing his coffee in two quick gulps.

"I don't expect you to handle this alone, Major. How many agents do you want to go with you?"

"None. I'll go alone."

The commander frowned. "That's a bad idea, Major. You'd be wise to take some backup with you."

Jack shook his head. "Several strangers arriving in Whitstable at the same time will draw undue attention. Let me go in alone. If I think I need help, I'll send word."

Commander Waterford stared at Jack for a long moment, then sighed. "Very well." He reached for a thin folder. "This is all the information we have. I hope there's something in there that helps you."

Jack rose to take the folder, briefly skimming the contents as he moved toward the door.

"One more thing, Washburn."

Jack turned at the door, staring at his commander's solemn expression. "Yes?"

"I may not be here when you return. I'm going to be at my daughter's in Lancaster. She just had a baby and wants me to come for the christening, then stay for a while."

"How long do you plan to be gone?"

"Not sure. A month or more. Depends on how bored I get."

"Who are they sending to take your place?"

"Commander Roger Levinson. Have you met him?"

Jack nodded. "We've met. Can't say we're friends."

"I'm not sure Levinson has friends."

"I can understand why," Jack said. "He's not an easy man to like."

"Trust no one," Waterford warned him as Jack walked out the door. "And try to come back alive."

Jack saluted his commanding officer and left the office.

He was glad he'd been sent on an assignment. If everything went as planned, Waterford would be back before Jack was. Then he and Levinson wouldn't even have to see each other.

JACK TRIED TO consider what he felt about the assignment. Two agents had already died, and it was possible that he might, too. He should be terrified. Or at least hesitant to go on such a dangerous assignment. But he wasn't.

The last several months had put a few things into perspective. Quinn and Theo, his two best friends and fellow soldiers, were both settled in their lives. They were happy being married and raising children.

That wasn't a possibility for Jack. He'd already found the love of his life and had lost her. He didn't want to search for another perfect woman. How could anyone compare to Annalise? She'd been as perfect as any woman could be. The only woman he would ever love.

But now she was dead.

He'd go on this assignment. If he came back alive, that would be the way it was supposed to be. If he didn't, that was also the way it was supposed to be. It didn't matter to him much either way. If he survived, there would always be another mission, and another. Until he went on a mission from which he didn't return.

Jack entered the boarding house where he kept a room. He couldn't call it the boarding house where he lived, because he didn't actually live there. His small flat on the third floor was only the room where he stored his clothes and slept when he didn't have anywhere else to sleep. When he wasn't sprawled in some pretty female's scented bed. This room in the boarding house was only the place he slept when he wanted to be alone, which wasn't often. Too many memories haunted his thoughts when he was alone. Thoughts and memories he didn't want to relive.

He climbed the stairs to the third floor and opened the door. There was no sense in calling this his home, because he didn't have a home. He hadn't had a home since Annalise killed herself.

Several letters lay scattered on the floor, and he picked them up and sifted through them. There were a few bills that he'd have to take care of before he left, but nothing important.

He was about to start packing when there was a knock at the door. Jack opened the door and had to lower his gaze to see the small, dirty lad in front of him.

"Here," the lad said, holding out a missive.

The boy was ready to run as soon as Jack took the letter. Instead of taking the letter, Jack grabbed the child's filthy collar and pulled him into the room.

"Let me go, you blighter!" the lad yelled. He struggled to get free, but Jack didn't release him.

He grabbed the letter and looked at it. There was nothing written on the outside of the hastily folded note.

"Who sent this?" he asked, still holding the youngster.

"I dunno," the boy answered. "I was just told to give it to ya."

"Was it a man or a lady?"

"Wasn't no lady, but it was a she."

"Young or old?"

"Young."

"Very well," Jack said, then reached in his pocket and took out a coin. The boy grabbed the coin and took off at a run. Jack let him go. He doubted the boy knew any more.

He stepped inside his room and closed the door behind him, then tore the missive open and scanned the writing. It was a woman's hand, but not an educated woman's writing. This person's penmanship was hardly legible.

He looked at the bottom of the letter, but there was no signature. Evidently, whoever wrote the letter didn't want to be recognized.

Jack poured some whiskey into a glass and carried it along with the note to the only chair in his flat and sat. He took a swallow and started to read the words in front of him.

It was difficult to make out all the words. The person's spelling was atrocious, and her sentences scarcely made sense. Thank heaven it wasn't long. Only four lines.

Magur,

Yor wife neds yu. Pleeze cum fast afor thay kil her

Shez not ded like yu think shez in the bilding behind the church in whitstable.

Hury

The paper dropped from his hand, and Jack watched it flutter to the floor. Although there was hardly a word that was spelled correctly, the meaning was clear. Annalise wasn't dead like he'd thought for the past two years. She hadn't killed herself, or drowned, like everyone wanted him to believe.

Without moving, Jack stared at the paper on the floor as if the words would change and his heart could start beating again. Then slowly, carefully, as if the paper was a priceless manuscript, he picked it up and read it again.

Annie was alive. The love of his life wasn't dead. So, what had happened to her?

Jack's temper rose. Why had she let him believe she was dead when she wasn't? What joke was she playing on him? And why?

What had made her put him through the hell he'd suffered over the last two years?

His blood roared in his head. His shock and disbelief turned to anger. Then fury. How could she have done something so cruel? She'd told him she loved him. People who loved each other didn't force them to go through hell.

Jack considered what he was going to do—go after her, or let her stay where she'd chosen to be.

He let the words in the missive echo again in his head.

Yor wife neds yu. Pleeze cum fast afor thay kil her

He threw more liquor to the back of his throat.

Yor wife neds yu. Pleeze cum fast afor thay kil her

Jack finished packing and stuffed the folder Waterford had given him in among his clothes. He went for his horse that he had stabled behind the boarding house and left.

He stopped at The Angel's Wings Jams and Jellies and told Milly that he didn't know when he'd be back. He left instructions that if she needed anything she should contact Theo, then left for Whitstable.

His brain had become a seething mess. Was he to believe that Annie wasn't dead? That she was still alive? And worse, that someone was trying to kill her?

He shook off his doubt. He had to operate as if it were all true. That she was being kept in the building behind the church in Whitstable. If he ignored it and was wrong, he'd never forgive himself.

Jack pushed Comet as fast as he dared and reached Whitstable in less than two hours instead of the usual three. The first thing he did was find the church, then go to the building behind it.

Jack stared at the run-down stone structure and the broken sign that read Whitstable Hospital. Several windows were cracked or were missing glass panes. Three stairs led to a worn gray porch where a half-dozen wooden chairs sat. An inside door to the building stood open, no doubt to allow a breeze to move the air inside, and the screen on the front sagged on its hinges. The lawn in the front was choked with weeds, and two flower-beds stood void of flowers.

Jack lifted his foot onto the first unsteady step. He hoped it would hold him.

After he climbed all three, he walked to the open door and stepped across the threshold. The interior of the hospital was no more inviting than the outside. In fact, it was considerably less hospitable.

If Annie had ever lived here, Jack didn't doubt that she was already dead.

CHAPTER TWO

JACK STOOD IN the foyer of the hospital and allowed his eyes to adjust to the darkness. There were no candles lit, nor were there any lamps aglow. Even the curtains at the windows had been closed and the draperies pulled. It was as if someone didn't want anyone to see inside the hospital.

"Hello," Jack called out, but no one answered. He called out again, then turned around, waiting for someone to answer his call.

It took a bit, but eventually he saw a man in a dark suit walking toward him.

"Welcome to Whitstable," the man said as a greeting.

The doctor wasn't at all what Jack expected. He was middle-aged and well built, but not very handsome. He appeared very muscular, more resembling a bodyguard, or a man hired to guard the door at a gaming hell than a man hired for his compassion or his medical training.

"Hello, doctor. My name is Jack—" Jack stopped. He thought it might be wiser to use a false name. "My name is Jack Lucas, but everyone calls me Jack."

"It's a pleasure to meet you, Jack. I'm Dr. Wintermere."

Jack smiled and extended his hand. "It's a pleasure to meet you."

"What brings you to Whitstable, Jack?"

"Nothing in particular. I'm just newly out of the service and have decided to spend several weeks traveling and getting reacquainted with the area before I'm forced to settle down and help my father run his business."

"And what business would that be?"

"He's a shopkeeper. He owns a jam and jelly shop in London."

"Oh, that sounds interesting."

"It is," Jack said. "But quite a bit more sedate than the life I was used to in the Army."

"I can imagine."

"Would you mind if I looked around your hospital?"

"Not at all, Jack. Let me show you. I insist."

"I'm sure I can manage on my own," Jack said.

"Please, I don't mind. Here, follow me."

Jack tried not to let his disappointment show. He would much rather have investigated on his own. He doubted Dr. Wintermere would take him where he was most interested in going.

"If you'll follow me," the doctor said, then led him down a long hallway, past one closed-off room after another. When they reached the end of the hall, they stopped.

"Do you mind if I look into some of the rooms?" Jack asked.

The doctor shook his head. "I'm afraid that's not permitted. We don't like disturbing our patients once we get them settled for the afternoon. I'm sure you understand how fragile many of them are."

"Yes, of course. What ailments do most of your patients suffer from?"

"Most of them suffer from mental deficiencies. Not all, of course, but many of them. Some of them have simply lost their memories and don't recognize their loved ones any longer. And some of them simply wander off and get lost. Their families can no longer keep them safe, so they entrust them to our care."

"I see."

Dr. Wintermere explained the history of the hospital, the special features of the rooms, and the number of staff members to care for the patients.

When he finished, he led Jack back to the waiting room. That's when Jack heard it.

The sound wasn't very loud, nor was it distinct enough that he could understand the muffled words being said, but it was definitely a sound made by a human. A high, keening cry of pain or torture.

"Did you hear that?" Jack asked.

"No, I didn't hear anything," the doctor said, attempting to lead him toward the door. "Nothing other than the creaks and heavy shifting of a crumbling old building."

"What does that door lead to?"

The doctor turned to where Jack pointed. "The cellar. But nothing is down there but spare beds and furniture and a few odds and ends. Nothing worth investigating."

Jack stopped to listen again. "Then I guess I couldn't have heard anything," he said, then turned to the exit. "Well, I've taken up enough of your time, Dr. Wintermere. Thank you so much for the tour."

"Thank you for your interest in our hospital. We're very proud of the work we do here."

Jack shot him a look. The doctoring would have to be a far sight better than the building maintenance if there were anything to be proud of.

"If you ever want another tour, come back. You're always welcome."

"Thank you," Jack said, and walked toward the exit. Although why anyone would want to return for another tour of empty hallways and rooms that were closed off to visitors, he had no idea.

"It was my pleasure," Dr. Wintermere said as Jack left the building.

There was something strange about the hospital. Something

strange about the noises he'd heard coming from what was described as the cellar. Something strange about Wintermere and how intent he was on steering Jack away from the cellar.

Jack mounted Comet and rode down the street until he was out of sight. He didn't want Wintermere to think he was overly curious about what went on at the hospital. Even though he was.

He'd have to come back later. After everyone was asleep for the night and he wouldn't run into anyone who might see him.

The first thing Jack was going to do was go to the boarding house he'd seen when he rode into town and get a room. He wasn't about to walk the streets until dark. That would only draw unwanted attention. He'd draw enough of that tomorrow or the next day, when the residents of Whitstable would see him out and about. Tonight he would do as much investigating as he could without anyone knowing.

Tomorrow he'd make himself known so the female who wrote the letter on Annie's behalf would know he'd come for her.

JACK GOT A room at a local lodging house and paid for two weeks. He hoped it wouldn't take him that long to find Annie, but he reminded himself that he'd been sent here on a mission. He was to uncover the ring of smugglers who were bringing in opium. That would no doubt take longer, and he didn't want the landlady to throw his clothes out onto the street if he happened to be gone more than a week.

He put the clothes he'd brought with him in a drawer and slid the bag under the bed. Then he took out his pistol and made sure it was loaded and ready to fire. He placed it on the bedside table within reach of the bed.

He didn't know why he expected trouble, but he did. Perhaps it was because two agents had already lost their lives trying to uncover who was in charge of the smuggling ring. But most likely, it was Commander Waterford's warning to watch his back that alerted him to the danger involved in this mission. He would have to be on his guard if he wanted to make it out of Whitstable alive.

Jack sat on the edge of the bed and took out the message again.

Yor wife neds yu. Pleeze cum fast afor thay kil her

Shez not ded like yu think shez in the bilding behind the church in whitstable.

Hury

Even though he had it memorized, he read it again. *Shez not ded. Shez not ded.*

When he first received word two years ago that Annie had taken her life, he didn't believe it. They were too much in love. Jack was happier being married to Annie than he'd ever been in his life. And he was convinced that she was happy, too.

So why had she jumped to her death?

That's what he'd been told. That was what Annie's stepmother had written him. She'd explained that Annie had been so miserable that she didn't want to live any longer. That because of his work as an agent for the government, she couldn't stand being left alone for such long periods of time. That Annie must have inherited her mother's mental sickness. Over time, she became so despondent and depressed that nothing they did for her helped her want to live. In the end, she took her own life.

Jack hadn't believed that lie at first. For two years he searched for her, but she wasn't to be found. Finally, he had to admit that what Annie's stepmother had written him was true, that his wife had been so miserable with him that she couldn't stand to live the life they'd forged together.

Jack rose from the bed and paced his room. He stopped on each pass past the window and looked out. The streets were quiet and there wasn't anything to see, but it was still too light to leave without drawing attention to himself. He couldn't go out until it was dark enough that no one would see him.

He paced the room several more times and tried to remember what Annie had looked like the last time he saw her. He could still see her golden hair and her blue eyes. He could still see her heart-shaped face and her ready smile. And if he allowed the memories to escape from where they were buried, he could still remember what it felt like to have her in his arms and hold her next to him. What it felt like to make love to her.

Jack sat in a cushioned chair and tipped his head back to rest it on the back of the soft chair. He closed his eyes and let his mind drift to his assignment.

What were the odds that the assignment he was sent on happened to be in Whitstable, Kent? And that was the same place where the message he'd received told him he'd find Annie?

What were the odds that he'd received the letter telling him that Annie was still alive the same day Waterford had sent him on a mission? And what did Waterford mean when he told him to watch his back and try to come back alive?

Jack considered the questions he didn't have answers to and listened until there wasn't any traffic going past. When it was dark enough outside that he wouldn't be seen, he left his room.

Whitstable was a quiet little town, barely larger than a village. Most of the men in the town worked the oyster beds, as their fathers and grandfathers had done before them, so their day began at dawn and ended at sundown. Jack hoped that meant no one would be out at this hour.

He made his way back to the hospital by a little-used path, and on foot, not wanting to draw attention saddling Comet. When he reached the hospital, he walked around the building to make sure the staff wasn't still about.

Everything was dark. The only sound he heard was the pounding of his heart. He couldn't believe it was possible he might see Annie again. Couldn't believe that in two years she hadn't been able to make her way to him. Or that she hadn't wanted to.

Fingers of dread wrapped around his heart and squeezed it unmercifully. The message had said she was in danger. Who would want to hurt her? Who would want her dead?

He kept close to the building as he made his way around the hospital. Finally, he reached an outside door that he hoped would lead him to the cellar. He tried the door, but it was locked.

He removed a knife from his pocket and pried the lock open, then stepped in. When he was safely inside, he lit the candle he'd brought with him and made his way down a flight of stairs.

The wooden steps were narrow and rotting, but he finally reached the bottom without mishap. He held his candle high and walked through the cellar. It was empty.

Jack's heart fell to the pit of his stomach. Was the note a prank? Had someone heard that he'd been married and that he wasn't any longer and decided to play a joke on him? Surely no one he knew would be that cruel.

He noticed a closed door in the corner of the cellar and pushed it open to check inside. It was the last place he had to look. He lifted his candle higher to look closer.

This room had a bed in it, and the bed had been slept in not that long ago. He walked around to the opposite side of the bed and looked down. A shawl had fallen onto the floor. He leaned over to pick it up and noticed a hairbrush with blonde hair tangled in it.

Jack's heart beat faster in his chest. His hands shook. He wanted to believe that Annie was alive, but it had been two years. For two years he thought she was dead. But what if she wasn't? What if she'd been alive all this time but had chosen not to return to him?

Jack picked up the brush and left the cellar. He closed and locked the door behind him and stayed in the shadows as he turned toward the street. He'd only taken a few steps when a voice stopped him.

"She ain't here no longer. They moved her."

Jack reached for the pistol in his pocket and spun to face his intruder. The female squeaked in fright, then pressed herself against the stone wall.

"Don't be afraid. I won't hurt you," he said.

Jack put the pistol back in his pocket and stepped closer to the female. She was small in stature, as if she hadn't eaten regularly, and her hair was a mousy brown, although it was combed neatly. Her clothes were worn, but looked clean from what Jack could see in the shadows. And she clutched her hands tightly at her waist as if she didn't trust him not to hurt her.

"Did you see where they took her?" he asked.

"I followed 'em."

"Can you show me?"

"Yeah, if you promise me you won't hurt her."

"I won't hurt her. You have my word."

She hesitated for several seconds, then lifted her gaze and looked at him. "Follow me."

They crept in the shadows until they reached an alley beyond the church, then crossed a meadow and went down another alley that led to the edge of the village. When they were nearly out of town, the girl motioned for Jack to stop, and he did.

"Were you the one who sent me the note?"

She nodded.

"What's your name?"

"Molly. Molly Dawes."

"Do you know who has her, Molly?"

She shook her head.

"Do you know why?"

She shook her head again. "All I know is that the head man says she's too much trouble now, and he says they can't afford to keep her around any longer."

"Have you ever seen this head man?"

Molly shook her head. "I only heard 'em talking and was afraid they were going to kill her, and I couldn't let them."

"Why?"

"'Cause I feel sorry for her. They haven't treated her very nice."

A knot twisted in Jack's stomach. So help him, he'd kill every one of them. "So where is she?"

"Through there," she said, pointing to a line of trees. "In that house."

"Is there anyone watching her?"

"At least two men. Maybe more."

"Are they armed?"

She nodded.

"You stay here, Molly. Don't follow me."

She nodded again, then stepped behind a tree to hide.

Jack removed his knife and gun from his jacket, then made his way to the small cottage where Annie was supposedly being held.

A single candle lit one room of the run-down cottage, and when he got near enough that he could look through a window, Jack saw the two men Molly had said were guarding Annie.

They sat in what looked to be the kitchen and were eating a meal of soup and bread. No one else seemed to be with them.

There was only one entrance to the cottage, the door that opened to the room where the two men were sitting. Jack didn't see weapons on the men, but that didn't mean they didn't have any. If they were sent to guard someone, they were most likely armed.

He made his way to the kitchen door, then kicked it open and aimed his gun at the table.

"Don't move. Either of you," he ordered, then took a step into the room.

Before Jack could turn around, a third man stepped out from the shadows and fired his pistol.

Jack ignored the burning in his shoulder and fired his gun. The man in the shadows went down and didn't move. Then Jack spun to face the two men at the table and fired at them.

They tipped the table over and used it to hide behind, then fired a round of bullets at him.

Jack dove behind one of the chairs in the room and fired, downing the second man. The other man stopped to reload his gun.

Jack wanted him alive. He wanted to know who was behind Annie's kidnapping. He needed to know if these men were connected to the opium smuggling he'd been sent to investigate.

Whitstable had been a smuggler's paradise during the Napoleonic Wars. He could imagine the same area being used to smuggle opium into England today.

While the gunman was reloading his pistol, Jack leapt across the room and tackled him to the ground. Even though he was the smallest of the kidnappers, he was surprisingly strong. The bullet in Jack's shoulder didn't help any, and the gunman took advantage of his wound.

Suddenly, the gunman pulled a knife out of his boot and lunged at Jack. Jack spun away, but the attacker slashed the weapon through the air. Jack had no choice but to defend himself the only way he could, and he stabbed the man in the chest with his own knife.

The man slid to the floor and lay without moving.

Jack leaned against the upturned table to catch his breath, then grabbed a cloth from the floor and wrapped it around his arm. He needed to stop the bleeding as soon as he could. He was getting weaker by the moment.

He took care of his wound, then lifted a candle from a nearby counter and went into the room where the third gunman had come from.

He held the candle high and noticed a bed in the room. There was a lamp on a small table beside the bed, and Jack lit it.

He lifted the lamp and illuminated the room enough that he could see that there was someone on the bed. But the person lay on her side, facing the wall, and he couldn't see her clearly.

It was a female. He could tell that. A female with light hair, but not golden blonde like Annie's. Nor was her body as lush and filled out as his wife's had been. This female was pale and painfully thin. This female hadn't been properly fed in a very long time.

Jack sat on the bed beside the prone figure and stared at the woman. She was breathing, but her breaths were shallow and labored. He doubted she was conscious. If she was aware of her surroundings, she'd decided to separate herself from what was happening to her. And he didn't blame her.

She'd been abused. How badly and for how long, Jack wasn't sure. She looked as if she hadn't been fed regularly, nor had anyone taken care of her. Her hair was unkempt and her hands were crusted with dirt. If this was Annie, it wasn't the Annie he knew. His Annie took immaculate care of herself. His Annie was a proud and particular female. Not at all like the woman lying on the bed.

Maybe it wasn't Annie. Maybe it was someone else. He almost hoped it was.

He placed his hand on her shoulder to turn her. He wanted to see her, wanted to know if this woman was his Annie, yet he was terrified that it was. Terrified that she'd been hurt more than he could help her recover from.

He slowly turned her over and stared at the woman lying on the bed.

His heart skipped a beat. His breath caught in his throat. The woman was Annie, and yet she wasn't. It was difficult to recognize her in the lamplight, but somehow in the gaunt, sunken cheeks he saw a hint of Annie. She'd been the love of his life—a beautiful, graceful, winsome beauty. She'd possessed his heart. But this broken creature didn't look at all like Annie. This woman was a stranger to him.

In the same moment that he was repulsed by her, his heart forced him to draw closer.

"Annie," he whispered as his eyes filled with tears. He slowly lifted her into his arms and held her. "Oh, Annie," he said as the first tear spilled. "What have they done to you?"

Jack held her like one would a small child and rocked her in his arms.

The tears refused to stop, and he let rivers of them fall for each day of the two years she'd chosen to stay away from him. He wanted and needed the tears to wash away the hurt and the anger he'd felt, because she'd broken his heart when she chose to leave him. All he wanted to know was why.

He wasn't sure how long he held her in his arms and rocked her. It might have been a matter of several minutes. It might have been an hour. Or perhaps it had been several hours. But every minute he held her in his arms, he became angrier.

If this was Annie, she had let him believe that she was dead. She'd stayed away from him even though she could have tried to escape. She hadn't even written him a note to tell him she wasn't dead.

Jack thought of all the months he'd searched for her. All the nights he drank to forget her and failed. The women he'd slept with as substitutes for his Annie.

He eventually realized that they weren't alone. He lifted his head and saw the girl Molly standing in the doorway.

"Is she dead?" she asked.

"No. And we're not going to allow her to die."

CHAPTER THREE

W HEN JACK'S LANDLADY saw him carrying a female to his room, she turned hostile. It took a great amount of explaining and an even greater amount of money to convince Mrs. Walters that Annie was his wife. She finally agreed to allow her to stay.

He rented three rooms indefinitely. One for himself, one for Annie, although he had no intention of allowing her to be alone, and one for Molly.

He also paid the landlady extra to cook special meals for Annie. Broth at first, and then some heartier soups. And he gave her extra coins to secure her silence and to send up some hot water so Annie could have a bath.

Cleanliness had always been important to Annie. She'd be horrified at the way she looked and smelled.

When the tub and the water arrived, Jack and Molly bathed Annie, then put her in one of Jack's shirts. He'd buy her some appropriate clothes when the shops opened in the morning. Until then, they'd get along with what he had with him.

"Are you sure you want me to stay here with the lady?" Molly asked after they'd bathed Annie. "I have a place where I can hide out for a while."

"No, I'll need you to help me with my wife when I have to be gone."

"Will she be all right?"

Jack wasn't sure how to answer Molly's question. "I don't know," he finally said, after propping Annie up in bed so he could feed her when Mrs. Walters brought up the broth she'd reluctantly agreed to heat in the middle of the night.

"How long has it been since you've seen her?" Molly asked.

"Two years," he answered.

"You have no idea what she went through. They kept moving us around. To awful, filthy, rat-infested places. We've only been here in Whitstable a few weeks."

Jack locked his gaze with Molly's. "Just a few weeks?"

"But Annie went mad long before we got here."

The word "mad" sent ice water coursing through Jack's veins. That had always been Annie's worst nightmare, that she'd go crazy just like her mother had. That she'd get to the point where she didn't know or recognize anyone, or even remember what she'd had for lunch a few hours before.

He refocused on Annie when the door opened and Mrs. Walters entered with a bowl of broth and some bread and cheese. "Thank you, Mrs. Walters," he said, then handed her another coin.

"Get her to eat as much as you can," the landlady said before she left the room. "She looks like she hasn't had a meal in a good long while."

"I'm afraid she hasn't," he answered on a sigh.

Thanks to the coins he'd given her, Mrs. Walters seemed to be warming to him. He hoped and prayed his money would last long enough to get Annie home.

"I can handle things from here, Molly," Jack said, preparing to feed Annie.

"Are you sure?"

"Yes. This may take a while. I don't know how well she'll cooperate."

"Very well," Molly answered, then rose and handed Jack a dark glass bottle.

"What is this?"

"It's the lady's medicine."

"Her medicine?"

"Yes. She'll be needing some before long. I'll bring up some wine before I go to my room. Just add a little to the wine and let her drink it. Not too much, though."

Jack pulled out the stopper on the bottle and held it to his nose. "How long has she needed this medicine, Molly?"

"Since before I started caring for her," she answered. "I was told she wouldn't survive if she didn't get her medicine, so I never forgot. Except for once, and she got terribly sick. I was afraid they were going to give me the boot, but they didn't. I never forgot her 'medicine' after that."

Jack set the bottle on the bedside table. "Thank you, Molly," he said before she left the room. But instead of thanking her, Jack wanted to lash out at her. What she was giving Annie was some of the most lethal and potent laudanum he had ever smelled.

"Annie?" he said, taking a spoonful of broth and lifting it to his wife's lips. At first she didn't react. He attempted to give her another spoonful of the broth, and this time she opened her mouth a crack—so he quickly tipped the spoon to the back of her mouth.

He tried again and again and was met with success about every other time he tried.

Finally, she opened her eyes and looked at him. Her gaze was hollow, the look on her face expressionless, as if she wasn't aware of her surroundings, or the reason she was here.

Jack experienced the first wave of apprehension, combined with dread. His wife's eyes were filled with cautionary mistrust. Everything about the way she glared at him indicated how suspicious she was of every movement he made. What he feared most was that if provoked, Annie would attack him. The very thought of being rough with her curdled his blood.

"Hello, Annie," he said, then lifted another spoonful of broth to her mouth. "I have something for you to eat," he said when her eyes narrowed and her gaze turned hostile.

She accepted the soup, then spat it at him and swung her arm through the air. Her fist connected with his jaw, and Jack clamped his fingers around her wrist to prevent her from hitting him again.

"Who the hell are you?" she screamed.

It took him several attempts to calm her, but nothing he tried seemed to work. She railed at him like a madwoman.

"What are you doing here?"

"I'm here to help you."

"No, you're not," she yelled, then attempted to escape from the bed.

Jack put the bowl of soup on the bedside table and trapped her on the bed. "Yes I am, Annie. You're safe now. No one can hurt you."

Her gaze darted around the room as if she were searching for someone.

"No one's here, Annie. Just us. You're safe."

"Where's my medicine?" she screamed. "I need my medicine."

She tried to escape again. Jack tried again to restrain her, but the harder he tried, the angrier she became. She fought him, kicked him, slapped him, and bit him. She called him more names than he thought his mild-mannered wife even knew, but her loudest and most forceful demand was for her medicine.

Her screams became more shrill and strident the longer she shrieked. She continued to fight to get off the bed.

Jack held her steady for a while, but eventually she escaped his grasp and jumped to her feet.

She ran to the nearest piece of furniture and emptied the drawers, throwing piece after piece of clothing to the floor.

"Where is it? What have you done with it?"

"What do you want, Annie?" Jack grabbed her hands to stop her from destroying the room.

She clawed at him until she drew blood. "Damn you! Give it

to me. I need it."

"What do you want?"

"Molly! Molly! Help me!"

"Stop, Annie! You'll wake everyone up! You'll get us thrown out on the street."

"Good! Help me! Somebody help me!" she screamed even louder.

"Annie, stop!"

"I need my medicine. I need my medicine!" She doubled over and clutched at her stomach. "Where's Molly? I need Molly!"

Jack gathered Annie in his arms, thinking he could calm her with his soft words. But nothing he did calmed her violent tremors. Even his firm hold and loving caresses didn't console her.

He wasn't sure whether it was the low, keening moans that came from the woman in his arms, the violent shivers that wracked her body, or her thrashing from side to side, but her trembling was unlike anything he'd seen before.

Her cries of pain grew louder and louder until Jack almost didn't hear the knock on the door.

He had Annie in his arms when Molly ran into the room. She poured a bit of wine in a glass, then added some of the "medicine" from the bottle in her hand to the wine and pressed it to Annie's lips.

Annie tried to hold the glass, but her hands trembled so violently that she couldn't. With practiced ease, Molly held the glass to her lips, and Annie eagerly took several swallows.

Molly gave her a few seconds to catch her breath, then let her drink some more.

"She'll be better soon," Molly said when the glass was empty. Then she held her mistress's hand in an attempt to calm her.

The effect from the "medicine" wasn't immediate, but gradual. Annie calmed. Her moaning stopped and her trembling eased. She curled in a ball on the bed and took several gulping breaths, then closed her eyes.

Jack pulled the covers over her and made her comfortable. When he finished, he stood at the side of the bed and stared at the woman who was his wife. A woman he barely recognized. He realized that he had just lived through the devastating effects of a person dependent on the poisonous drug opium.

"Don't leave me, Molly," Annie said groggily. "You can never leave me again."

The young girl took Annie's hand and held it. "I won't, mistress. I won't leave you. Now go back to sleep. It's too early to rise. The sun's not even up yet. Mrs. Walters will be bringin' you something to eat for breakfast. That will make you feel better."

"I'm not very hungry this morning, Molly."

"You will be when you smell what Mrs. Walters brings for ya. She's a mighty fine cook, she is."

Annie looked up, and her gaze locked with Jack's. She pulled away from him as if his eyes burned her. There was no love in her gaze. No friendship. Only bitterness and distrust.

"Who are you?" she whispered.

"I'm Jack."

"No, you're not!"

"I am. And I've come to take you home."

"No! Get away from me," she yelled. "Don't touch me."

Jack pulled a cover up over her. "Annie," he whispered. "It's me. Jack."

"No! Jack's dead."

"No. I'm right here. I came to take you home."

"No!"

Her actions turned violent again, and he had a difficult time controlling her.

"Don't let him take me, Molly! He'll lock me up. Don't let him do that to me!"

"I won't, mistress. I won't let him take you away. I'll be right here. You'll be fine."

Annie smiled. Her grin was one of gratitude and thankfulness. But not for him. For Molly.

"Thank you, Molly," she slurred.

"Go back to sleep, mistress. I'll be right here when you wake."

Annie turned her head, and her gaze again locked with Jack's. "Why are you here?" she asked him, as if she couldn't understand why he would come after her.

"Because I've missed you."

A frown furrowed her forehead. "Why?"

"Don't you remember?"

She stared at him with a puzzled expression.

"We used to be married. We lived on an estate called Burnhaven. Do you remember it?"

"Burnhaven?"

"Yes."

"I remember Burnhaven. I wanted to go back there, but they wouldn't let me."

"Who wouldn't let you, Annie?"

She looked around the room as if making sure no one could overhear her. "The men who locked me away," she whispered. "They wouldn't let me leave."

"Why wouldn't they?"

"Because of the land."

"What land, Annie?"

"The land my father gave me."

Jack frowned. "I didn't know your father had any land."

"Yes, he did. I don't know exactly where it is, but he wants it. He tried to make me sign it over to him, but I wouldn't do it."

"So, he locked you up so you'd give him the land?"

Annie lifted her gaze and looked at Jack. He saw the glassy emptiness in her gaze. The laudanum had taken effect.

"I don't want to talk about this anymore."

"Very well. We won't."

Jack sat in the chair beside Annie's bed and watched her sleep. Molly lay beside Annie and slept, too.

He wasn't sure how long he sat there and watched his wife

sleep. She barely moved. Her breathing was slow and steady, as if the poison she'd ingested had put her in a sleep so deep she was nearly unconscious.

The woman before him didn't resemble the one he'd married. This woman's youth and vitality had been stolen from her. This Annie's zest for life and living was no longer evident. It had been taken from her, the same as her ready smile and infectious laughter.

There was nothing left of the girl he'd married. Nothing that he recognized of the female he'd loved so fiercely.

His heart grew heavy and his eyes filled with water. He closed his eyes, but not before one tear after another spilled over his lashes and ran down his cheeks.

He had lost the love of his life. He only prayed he'd be able to find a way to get her back.

JACK TRIED TO sleep, but sleep wouldn't come. He didn't know how long it had been before there was a knock at the door.

He rose and let Mrs. Walters enter with a breakfast tray. "Thank you, Mrs. Walters," he said as she left the plate with warm, soft foods on the bedside table near Annie and exited the room.

As if Molly sensed she was needed, she woke and sat on the edge of the bed beside Annie, who opened her eyes and sat up.

"Would you stay with your mistress for a bit while I go to buy her something to wear?" he asked.

"Of course, Major."

"Get Mrs. Walters if you have any trouble, Molly."

"I won't, Major. As soon as Annie eats a little something, she'll take a nap, won't you, Annie?"

"Can I have more of my medicine, Molly?" Annie asked.

"Just a little."

"Thank you, Molly," she said, then ate a spoonful of the food Mrs. Walters had brought up.

"If I can locate a doctor, I'm going to bring him back with me," Jack said.

"No! I don't want to see a doctor."

"I know you don't, but I'd feel better if you were looked at by a doctor. Do it for Molly, will you?"

Annie looked at Molly, who nodded her agreement.

"Very well," she agreed, but Jack could tell she was reacting by rote. She wasn't really thinking things through, only saying what she thought Molly wanted her to say. This was not at all like the Annie he had married.

"I won't be long, Annie. Molly will take good care of you. And if you'd like, I'll bring you back a sticky bun. I remember how fond you were of them."

"Oh, yes. And bring one for Molly, too."

"Yes, I will."

Jack touched her cheek, but she pushed his hand away. She wanted nothing to do with him. He wondered if she would ever remember how much they'd loved each other. How much they'd meant to each other. Mostly he wondered if it was possible for them to ever be that way again.

Annie ate a little more of her breakfast, then curled herself into a tight ball and lay with her back to him. "I'm tired. I need to sleep."

"Yes, you get some rest. I'll be back in an hour or so."

He looked at Molly as if searching for answers, but she had none to give him, so he opened the door and stepped out into the hall.

"Jack?"

"Yes, Annie?" he said, stepping back into the room.

"Do you have our baby?"

His heart skipped a beat, and he clenched his hand to the door frame to hold himself steady. "What did you say?"

"Do you have our baby?"

"No, Annie. I don't have our baby."

Annie became visibly agitated. Tears sprang to her eyes and ran down her cheeks. "Someone took her, and I don't know where they have her. Would you help me find her?"

Jack swallowed past the lump in his throat. "Yes, Annie. I'll help you find her."

Annie lay back down and closed her eyes.

※

CHAPTER FOUR

Jack stepped into the hall and closed the door behind him. Once he was alone, his legs buckled beneath him and he sank to the floor.

Annie had a baby. She had a little girl and she couldn't find her. Whether someone had taken her, or she was imagining it, or the baby had never existed, he didn't know. But if she had a child and it was still alive, he wouldn't rest until he found her. He wouldn't stop looking until he knew where his daughter was.

After several heart-wrenching minutes, Jack pushed himself to his feet and left the lodging house. He went to a local clothing shop and purchased anything he thought Annie would need. Then he walked to a pastry shop and bought several sticky buns and a variety of other pastries. His wife needed to eat. She'd lost too much weight and needed to get her strength back.

When he paid for the pastry items, he asked the clerk if Whitstable had a doctor. The clerk directed Jack to Dr. Reynolds' office.

He followed the directions the clerk gave him and entered the doctor's office a short while later.

"May I help you?" an elderly woman neatly dressed in white asked him.

"Is the doctor in?"

"Yes, but he's with a patient. If you'd like to wait, he should be free in a few minutes. Just have a seat."

"Thank you," Jack said, and took a seat.

The hands on the clock didn't seem to move fast at all, but finally the doctor came out of his office assisting an elderly woman to the door. When the lady was gone, the doctor turned to Jack.

"Can I help you?" he asked.

Jack looked at the doctor, who wasn't at all what he'd expected. He expected to find an elderly doctor who had years of experience in a sleepy town such as Whitstable. Instead, the man standing in front of him couldn't be more than thirty at the most. He was tall and muscular, and had a pleasing smile that put Jack at ease before he said a word.

"Could we talk?"

"Of course," the doctor answered. "Come with me."

Jack followed the doctor into his office and waited until he'd closed the door before he spoke. "Dr. Reynolds?"

"Yes. What can I do for you?"

"I have a rather delicate matter I'd like you to help me with."

"And that is?"

"Perhaps you could look at my shoulder while I explain."

Jack removed his shirt, and the doctor examined his shoulder. He took one look and his eyes widened. "This is a bullet wound," he said in surprise. "And from the look of your shoulder and back, it's not the first one you've taken."

"No," Jack said. "I was in the war."

"Except the war is no longer raging."

"No, it isn't," Jack said, but offered no other explanation.

The doctor probed the wound, and Jack winced.

"I've already removed the bullet," Jack explained. The doctor gave him a second look, and Jack smiled. "I just need you to put something on it to keep it from getting infected."

The doctor reached for what he needed to clean Jack's wound. "Is this the matter you wanted to discuss?"

"No."

"If this isn't the delicate matter you wanted to discuss, I can't wait to hear what that might be."

Jack smiled. He'd taken an instant liking to this doctor. "It's my wife," he said. "You're going to find this strange, but—"

The doctor lifted his gaze and gave Jack a questioning look. "Why do I think there is nothing about you that isn't a bit…strange, Mr….?"

"Washburn. Jack Washburn."

"Mr. Washburn," the doctor repeated. "And you can call me Jonah, Jack. I have a feeling we're going to become acquainted enough to be on a first name basis."

"I have a feeling you're right," Jack said as the doctor worked on his shoulder.

"Now, about your wife?"

"My wife was kidnapped close to two years ago and at some point was brought here," he explained. "I just found her yesterday. She's been held captive. I'm not sure why."

"But you have an idea?"

"Yes. I have an idea."

"But you cannot say what that reason is?"

"Not yet. All I know is that to keep her quiet and sedate enough that she didn't cause any trouble, her captives gave her a steady dose of laudanum."

"How long has she been given laudanum?"

"I'm not sure, but I assume the better part of two years."

The doctor finished bandaging Jack's shoulder and handed him his shirt. "That's long enough," Jonah said.

"Long enough for what?"

"To become dependent on it."

Jack closed his eyes and held them shut for several moments. "Yes, I'm sure she's dependent on laudanum. I tried to skip the dose she usually has at bedtime, and she suffered a violent reaction."

"That would be common," Jonah said. "Did you need me to stop in to see her?"

"Yes, if you would. But I have her in hiding so whoever kidnapped her won't find her."

"I'll wait until after I close my office then come to see her."

"She's at Mrs. Walters' boarding house. On the third floor at the end of the hall."

"I'll find it. Will you need a supply of laudanum, or do you have enough on hand?"

"I will need some, but I was told I can get it at any apothecary."

"Yes," the doctor agreed, "but if you are trying to keep your wife hidden from whoever kidnapped her, they'll be watching for anyone purchasing a fresh supply of laudanum. She'll be safer if I get it for you."

"Thank you," Jack said. He gathered his things and went to the door. "I'll see you tonight, then."

"Yes. I'll be there after dark. Have you decided how you're going to handle her dependency?" the doctor asked before Jack could leave.

"I was hoping you would explain our options and Annie and I could decide what would be best. I can't be in a hurry to begin the process, though. I have to find the men who are smuggling opium into Whitstable and selling it."

"Is that your mission?"

"That's the reason I'm here. Yes."

"Do you work for the government, Jack?"

He hesitated, not sure how much he was wise in divulging. Somehow, he was sure he could trust Reynolds. If he was wrong, he was putting several lives in danger.

"I'm a special agent for the Crown, although I'd appreciate your discretion. The reason I'm here isn't a matter I want broadcast far and wide."

"I can understand that. And I agree. I'm sure the men smuggling opium into Britain would not like to see their profits diminished."

"And from the looks of it, it's quite a lucrative business," Jack said.

"I should have known there was a reason I've had to treat more and more patients with symptoms of opium use. Now I understand why. It has become too readily available."

"Yes. There's a smuggling operation going on in Whitstable."

"Do you know who is leading this smuggling operation?"

Jack shook his head. "Not yet, but I have every intention of uncovering its leader."

"And I will help in any way I can. The use of laudanum is still considered an acceptable treatment for anyone with mild ailments, from coughs to colds to headaches to severe ailments."

"But you don't consider it acceptable?"

"No. I've seen the effects on patients who are dependent on opium, which is what laudanum contains. Even to the point of death."

"So have I," Jack said. "In the war. Too many of our soldiers came back with a dependency to the drug. If they came back at all."

"I have treated several of those, too."

"I imagine you have."

"I will see you this evening. Will your wife be up to seeing me?" Jonah asked.

"She won't like it, but I will tell her you're coming."

"It's natural for a patient who is dependent on laudanum not to want me to treat them. What they fear most is that I'll take their laudanum away from them. The drug is very powerful, and anyone who has taken it as long as you think your wife has will have a strong desire to continue to take it."

Jack agreed with Dr. Reynolds. He'd seen proof of that last night. "But I should warn you of something first."

"Yes?".

"For some reason, my wife doesn't trust me. She's very angry with me."

"It's possible she fears you intend to take her opium away from her. You are a threat to her. Just as I will be at first. Until she learns to trust us."

"Yes, she told me as much."

"That is every person's most monumental fear. That someone close to them intends to take their 'medicine' away from them. Once they are dependent on their medicine, they'll do everything in their power to keep it within easy reach."

"Until tonight," Jack said, then left.

He walked down the street to the boarding house, keeping a watchful eye on his surroundings. He wanted to make sure no one was following him. He took several turns in an effort to avoid being followed, and several minutes later entered the boarding house and went up the stairs.

The landlady was just coming from Annie's room. "Good day, Major Washburn."

"Good day, Mrs. Walters. How are you this morning?"

"Very well, thank you. I just took a tea tray to your wife. She seems much improved this morning."

"Yes," Jack answered. "No doubt because of your excellent broths. She ate them with much enthusiasm."

"I'm glad to hear that."

"I brought her a pastry. Would you like one before they're gone?"

"I would indeed," she answered, then took one from the paper package Jack opened.

"I wonder if you might have a back entrance I can use to enter your lodgings? There are times when I don't want my comings and goings watched."

"I do, Major. It's an entrance from the alley behind the house. It will bring you in through the kitchen and up these stairs right here. I usually keep the door locked, but I can't see where it would hurt to let you have a key." She reached in her pocket and pulled out a string with a metal key attached to it.

"Thank you, Mrs. Walters. You've been most helpful."

"You're quite welcome."

Jack turned away, then stopped. "By the way, Dr. Reynolds

will be stopping by this evening. Would you show him up when he arrives?"

"I'll be sure to send him right up," the landlady said, then left.

Jack put his key in the door then entered his room. Annie was alone in the chair near the window, drinking a cup of tea.

"I'm just in time," he said, then handed her a sticky bun.

"Oh," she said excitedly. "I haven't had a sticky bun in ever so long."

"I knew you hadn't, so I brought you two of them."

"Oh!"

He placed the package with the sticky bun and other pastries on a plate Mrs. Walters had left. Annie took a bite of the bun and licked her lips.

"Oh, this is delicious," she said. "I forgot how scrumptious they are."

Jack sat down on a chair close to Annie and poured himself a cup of tea, then took a pastry from the bag. "Can we talk?" he asked.

"No," Annie said while she ate her sticky bun. "I don't want to talk about what happened to me."

"Why not?"

"Because I don't remember some of it."

"What do you mean by that?"

"Too much happened that I don't remember."

"How can you not remember what happened to you, Annie?"

"I just don't," she snapped.

Jack watched as she closed herself off from him. "What are you afraid of, Annie?"

"I'm not afraid of anything. Why would you think I'm afraid?"

He backed off from questioning her. She had become defensive. She'd become protective. And afraid.

Of him?

"I just want to understand what you went through."

"I don't want to talk about it, Jack. You don't need to know what happened."

"Wouldn't you like to tell me?"

"No." She rose from the chair and paced the room nervously, wrapping her arms around her waist and clutching her hands tightly. "I want my medicine, Jack. Where is it?"

"I'm not sure, Annie."

"I want my medicine! Where's Molly?"

As if Molly had heard, she rapped on the door and came into the room.

"Molly," Annie said excitedly. "Where's my medicine? I need my medicine."

"'Tis right here, mistress. I'll get it for you."

Annie paced the room while Molly poured a few drops of laudanum into a glass of wine. When it was mixed, she gave it to Annie, who greedily drank it. She set the glass down and sat on the edge of the bed.

Jack watched as she rocked back and forth, back and forth.

Molly placed her arm around Annie's shoulders and held her close. Jack couldn't take in how this had happened. Molly comforted Annie as if Annie was the child and Molly was the adult. As if Molly was the caregiver and Annie the child needing care.

"Are you tired now, mistress?"

"Yes. I'm terribly tired. I'd like to rest now."

Molly helped Annie get under the covers, then stroked her brow until she fell asleep.

Jack waited until he was sure Annie was asleep, then walked to the door. He motioned for Molly to follow him out into the hall, then closed the door after her.

He stepped a few feet away from the door so Annie couldn't hear them, then turned to Molly.

"When did you first meet Annie?"

"About a year and a half ago."

"Was she with child when you first met her?"

Molly lowered her gaze, then nodded. "I think that's why

they wanted me to stay with her."

"Who were they?"

"The men who brought her here."

"Did you hear their names?"

She shook her head. "No."

"Why did they want her?"

"I don't know. I think it had something to do with some land."

"Some land? Where was this land?"

"I don't know. I only know they wanted the land and Annie wouldn't give it to them."

"When you stayed with Annie did you help her take her medicine?"

"Yes. She didn't want to take it, though. She fought real hard not to take it, but they made her."

Jack knew he had to ask about the babe, had to find out what happened to her. He wouldn't rest until he knew. He was desperate to get his daughter back, desperate to know what had happened to her.

"What happened to the child she had?"

Molly refused to look him in the eyes. She lowered her chin and stared at the floor.

"What happened to the babe, Molly?"

"I don't know. She was with us when we fell asleep one night, and the next morning she was gone."

"Gone where?"

"I don't know. She was just gone."

Jack could tell Molly felt guilty for letting Annie's baby get taken away from her, that she considered it her fault. But he wanted her to know he didn't blame her.

"It wasn't your fault. You couldn't watch the baby day and night."

"But if I hadn't fallen asleep..." she said.

"Don't, Molly. What's done is done. Now, go to bed. You don't have to wait up with Annie. I'll be here. I'll watch over her.

Dr. Reynolds promised to drop by later on."

"Does the mistress know Dr. Reynolds is coming?"

"No. Does that matter?"

"She doesn't like doctors. She doesn't trust 'em."

"We'll be careful, then, not to upset her."

Molly nodded, then walked to her room and opened the door. "Call if you need me."

"I will," he answered. "Thank you."

Jack considered how attached Molly was to Annie and wondered if their connection meant something. He wondered if someone was paying Molly to watch over Annie and decided he needed to watch her closer.

None of this made sense.

CHAPTER FIVE

ANNIE OPENED HER eyes and looked at Jack sleeping in the chair beside her bed. She hadn't intended to sleep as long as she had.

She studied the man who was her husband. She'd hoped he would never come after her, but somehow he'd found her. She wondered how. Someone must have told him. She wondered who.

Yet she knew. It had to have been Molly.

She wished the girl hadn't told him.

Annie rolled to the other side of the bed and got to her feet. She straightened her clothes and combed her hair, then sat on the edge of the bed and watched Jack sleep.

He was still as handsome as he'd ever been. Still as mesmerizing as when she'd first met him. And she still loved him as much as she always had. And always would. But she couldn't let him know that. She wasn't worthy of his love. She wasn't worthy of any man's love.

She wasn't the same person he'd married. She didn't deserve to be with him, not like she was now. He was still perfect. She was not.

Tears filled her eyes and threatened to spill over her lashes. She wished she could return to the day before she'd been ruined, return to the day when she was happy, but those days were just a dream now. It was too late to go back. Far too late.

She had to leave him. She had to get away from him so she wouldn't ruin his life. He deserved so much more than her. He deserved a wife like she once was, before she'd taken laudanum that first time.

She swiped the tears from her eyes and looked up to see him watching her.

"You're awake," she said.

"Yes. I'm awake." Jack threw the covers off and sat beside her on the edge of the bed. "Did you sleep well?"

"Yes."

"I've invited a friend to come see us," he said.

"Who?"

"His name is Jonah Reynolds. He's a doctor."

"No! I don't want to see a doctor. You can't make me!"

Jack rose to take control of Annie's outburst, but stopped when a knock sounded at the door. He went to open it.

"Jonah, please, come in and meet my wife."

"I don't need you here," Annie said angrily. "I don't want you to be here."

"That's understandable, Mrs. Washburn," Dr. Reynolds said. "Actually, I didn't come to see you. I came to see your husband."

She looked at him as if she didn't believe him, but she sat back in her chair and let the doctor take a seat beside Jack.

"Would you like a brandy?" Jack said.

"Let's have a look at your shoulder first."

"What's wrong with your shoulder?" Annie asked. She hadn't realized he'd been injured or that anything was wrong with his shoulder.

"I had a little accident, and Jonah looked at it earlier."

The doctor rose and opened his bag. He took out a small jar of salve and several clean bandages while Jack removed his shirt.

"You've been shot!" she cried.

"It's nothing. Jonah took good care of me already."

Annie remained where she was and watched the doctor take

care of Jack's shoulder. She still didn't believe the doctor's primary reason for coming was to take care of her husband, but they both were convincing her it was true.

The longer the doctor chatted, the more desperate Annie was to have a dose of her medicine. The longer she had to go without her medicine, the more she needed it.

She walked over to the dresser where Molly kept the laudanum and opened the top drawer.

It wasn't there.

She moved the few clothing items around but couldn't find what she was looking for.

Annie's searching became more frantic. Her skin crawled with the need of her medicine. Jack knew she needed it and was trying to embarrass her in front of the doctor. He'd hidden it on purpose. How dare he? She hated him for what he was doing to her.

She turned to face him. "Where did you hide it?"

"Hide what, Annie?"

"You know damn good and well," she yelled, and threw an unlit candle at him. "Where is it?"

He rose and walked toward her. "What is it you're looking for, Annie?"

"My medicine!"

Jack turned to the drawer and moved a few items of clothing around. "Is this what you're looking for, Annie?" He held out her bottle of laudanum, and she grabbed it from his hand.

He poured a small portion of wine into a glass, then calmly took the bottle of laudanum from her and added a few drops to the wine. He gave it a stir, then handed it to her.

Annie should be embarrassed, but she needed her medicine too badly to feel anything but a desperation to drink the wine.

"How long have you needed to take your medicine?" the doctor asked a little while after Annie had returned to her chair.

"I don't *need* to take it," she argued. She knew he was insinuating that she was dependent on her medicine, but she wasn't.

She could stop taking it anytime she wanted. She simply didn't *want* to stop. She needed it for the way her head ached at times. And to calm herself. And to help her stop shaking.

"Would you ever want help learning to live without your medicine?"

"Why would I want to quit taking it? I need it."

"What if I told you that you don't need it?"

"Stop it! I don't want to listen to you anymore."

"I'm sorry if I upset you," Jonah said.

The doctor wasn't sorry he'd upset her. This was the reason he'd come. Jack had asked him to come so he could evaluate her. He wanted the doctor to tell him if he thought she could be freed of her desire for the opium she'd been taking for almost two years. He wanted to know if there was hope for her to change back to the woman he'd married.

Jack wanted the doctor's opinion so he could decide if it was worth staying married to her. Or if he should divorce her.

"Don't think I don't know what you are doing, Jack. I do. You had your friend come so he could tell you what he thought. So he could tell you if he thought your wife could be cured."

"That's not true, Annie," Jack said. "I asked Jonah to come so he could meet you. So he could talk to you. So he could find out *if* you wanted help."

She shot Jonah a harsh glare. "Well, doctor. What have you concluded? Do I want help?"

"No, Annie," he replied. "You don't want help."

She turned her attention back to her husband. "Did you hear him, Jack? I don't need help."

"That's not what Jonah said, Annie. He said that you aren't ready to be helped yet. Not that you don't need help."

Annie reached for her glass of wine and brought it to her mouth. But it was empty.

She set it back on the table with a thud. "I'm tired," she said, and went into the connecting room Jack had rented for her and shut the door.

JACK GAVE ANNIE enough time to get ready for bed and fall asleep, then opened her door and checked on her. When he was sure she was asleep, he returned to his room.

"What do you think?" he asked Jonah.

"She's a perfect example of someone who is dependent on opium. She can't get along without it, yet denies she needs it."

"What do you suggest I do?" Jack was at a loss as to how to cure Annie of her reliance on laudanum. This was his wife they were talking about. This was the woman with whom he'd fallen in love. This was the woman he still loved. But she wasn't the same woman she'd been two years ago. She'd changed so much Jack didn't even recognize her. He wanted the woman he'd married back. Not the woman she'd become.

"I wish I could offer you more hope," Jonah said, "but in her condition, I'm afraid I can't. The main problem you're facing is her denial that she has a problem."

Jack raked his fingers through his hair. "I know," he said. "I heard her. She doesn't think she needs the laudanum, yet you saw how frantic she became when she couldn't find her 'medicine.'"

"The fact that she refers to her laudanum as 'medicine' is another indication that she considers it something she can't get along without."

"What do you suggest we do?" Jack asked.

"My suggestion right now is to do nothing. The more you try to pressure her, the more adamant she'll become. She's the one who has to decide when she wants help. She's the one who will have to decide when she's lost more because of the laudanum than she's benefited from it."

"What if she doesn't?"

"Let's cross that bridge when we come to it," Jonah said, then took a swallow of his brandy. "This mission you're on, Jack. Do you have any idea yet who you're looking for?"

Jack shook his head. "First I need to discover where they're bringing their opium ashore. They've got to have a place along the coast where they unload their cargo."

"There are a lot of miles of shore to cover."

"I know. I intend to go out tomorrow and begin the search."

"I'd volunteer to go along with you if I had a free day, but I don't."

"Don't worry. I might be at this for a while."

"No doubt."

Jack and Jonah talked for several minutes more, then Jonah rose to leave. "Here," he said, reaching into his pocket. He took out several vials of laudanum and handed them to Jack. "Hide them where she won't find them."

Jack nodded.

"She must not get her hands on them when she's desperate. She won't realize how much she's taking and could take too much. And that could be fatal."

"I didn't realize how dangerous laudanum was."

"No one does. The doctors still prescribe it for almost everything that ails their patients. You can purchase laudanum in almost every dry goods store, apothecary, or anywhere that sells a tonic of any sort."

"I wish the authorities would stop its sale," Jack said. "But they won't. Because laudanum is not banned for use in England, the sale of the elixir is legal."

"Things are changing," Jonah said. "I've seen a rise in the number of citizens who are in the same condition as your wife."

"That's because the smugglers are bringing high-grade opium from Turkey into the country. It's only drawn the government's attention because they're smuggling it in without paying Her Majesty her share of the profits. The fact that they smuggle their contraband into the country without paying the government the taxes they owe is the only reason the government wants the smuggling stopped."

"Hopefully, the day will come when the authorities realize

the harm opium is doing our citizens and outlaw its sale," Jonah said.

"We can only hope," Jack muttered as he walked Jonah to the door.

When the doctor was gone, Jack hid the laudanum where he was certain Annie wouldn't find it. Then he sat down and wrote his two fellow agents, and closest friends, Quinn and Theo, and asked them for their help in taking down the smuggling ring.

No one was better at ferreting out a band of lawbreakers than his fellow special agents, even though they didn't work for the government any longer. There was no one Jack trusted more than Quinn and Theo to help him find the bastard who had caused Annie to become reliant on the drug that had ruined her life. And his.

Jack had to find the person responsible and put him away. And he could not fail. Annie's life depended on it.

And so did his.

⇶⫷

JACK WOKE EARLY the next morning and dressed for the day. He waited until Annie stirred, then went to the room where she slept. She was just waking.

"What are you doing?" she asked in an accusing tone.

"I have some letters to put in the post, then I intend to go to the ocean and search the coastline."

"Who did you write to?"

"I wrote to Quinn and Theo."

"Why did you write to them?"

"I want them to come and help me locate the smugglers."

"Do you think you'll find them?"

"There's a lot of coastline to cover. I doubt I'll find where they're bringing in the contraband the first day. But I don't intend to give up until I do."

"What do you expect me to do while you're gone all day?"

"When I rode into town, I noticed that Whitstable has a bookstore. You used to like to read. I'll stop by the shop and buy you some books."

Her eyes shone with a glimmer of interest and her features softened. He was glad. She looked more like the Annie he remembered.

"And I'll pick you and Molly up some pastries before I leave for the coast. Would you like a sticky bun again this morning, or are you getting tired of them?"

"No," she said firmly. "I doubt I'll ever get tired of them."

"No. I doubt you will." Jack shrugged on his jacket and walked to the door. "Mrs. Walters will be here with your breakfast before long, and I'll make sure Molly is with you before I leave."

"Can I go to the bookstore with you?" she asked before he had the door open."

"No, Annie. You can't. The men who were holding you captive will be looking for you. They know you can't have gone far, so they will be scouring Whitstable for you."

The glare in her eyes hardened. He knew it was the drug that caused her to want to argue with everything he suggested. He knew it was her distrust of him, and that distrust was centered around her fear that he would take away her supply of laudanum. He was her enemy. He represented everything she feared.

"I'll send Molly in to be with you."

She turned her head so she didn't have to look at him.

A nagging pain settled around his heart. This wasn't what he remembered of the love they'd once shared. The love he remembered had been an all-consuming one; they accepted and forgave every part of each other.

That wasn't what he saw in Annie's actions or the look on her face. What he saw now was a wariness that refused to go away.

Jack left the room and knocked on Molly's door. "Good morning, Molly."

"Good morning, Major."

"I have a few errands to run, then I'll return with some pastries for your mistress and yourself. Lock the door the minute I leave and don't open it for anyone except me or Mrs. Walters."

"Yes, Major."

Jack handed Molly a vial of laudanum and watched her put it in her pocket. He waited until she was with Annie and he heard the door lock, then he left.

He walked down the three-block main street and entered the bookstore he'd seen when he first arrived in Whitstable. The shop wasn't large, and it didn't take him long to find several books he thought Annie would like. His next stop was the bakery for a supply of pastries and sticky buns.

As he was walking back to their lodgings, he saw a shop that had a large selection of hard candies. He couldn't resist the urge to buy a sack of candy for Annie, and another for Molly.

As he was leaving the shop, he walked past a selection of stationery and writing utensils. He picked up some paper and a pencil and bought it. He wasn't sure why, but he thought perhaps writing a letter or two might occupy Annie's time. He wasn't sure to whom he thought she would write. Everyone she was close to thought she was dead. Hearing from her would be a big shock to them.

When he finished, he gathered his purchases and took them back to Annie.

"What did you buy?" she asked when he entered the room.

The look in her eyes told him that she'd recently taken her medicine. Although he preferred her calm state of mind after she'd taken laudanum, he knew that the reverse would happen when its effects wore off.

"I got you some sticky buns," he said, handing her the wrapped pastries. "And some books." She perused the titles and squealed with delight at each one. "And, as a special treat, I bought you and Molly each a bag of candy."

Jack wasn't sure who was more excited about the sweet treat,

Annie or Molly.

"Oh, Major. Thank you," Molly squealed with delight, then sat in one of the chairs, looked through her bag of candy, and chose her first piece.

"And this is a special gift for you, Annie." He reached in the package and took out the writing paper and the pencil.

Annie's eyes filled with tears. "What's this for, Jack? I don't need writing paper. I don't know anyone I'd even write to."

"I do," he said. "Perhaps you could write to our daughter and tell her how much you miss her. And you could tell her about me. She's never even seen me, so she doesn't know anything about me. You could tell her that I'm looking for her and I won't stop until I find her. And when I do, that we're going to take her home. And then you could tell her about her home. What it looks like, and that she'll have her own room with a bed of her own and a doll to sleep with."

"Stop it," Annie said as tears streamed down her cheeks. "We don't even know if she's still alive."

"Yes, we do," he said forcefully. "I refuse to think that she's not. She's alive. She has to be."

Annie wiped her tears. "Yes, she's alive," she said. "She has to be. We can't think that she's not."

"No, Annie. We can't."

Jack gathered Annie's hands in his and held them. This was the Annie he'd married. The Annie he loved.

"I have to go now. I'll be back before dark. Look through your books and decide which one you're going to read first," he said, then walked to the door. "Lock the door behind me, Molly."

"Yes, Major."

Jack went to the stable to get his horse, then rode to the shore.

It was a beautiful day, and he enjoyed riding along the coast. He traveled several miles, stopping to investigate every cave that looked as though it was large enough to hide the contraband the smugglers were bringing ashore. But his searching turned up nothing.

When the sun started to go down, he made his way back to Whitstable and returned to the boarding house. Mrs. Walters had already brought up their dinners and Annie and Molly had begun to eat. He was glad. There was no sense in their waiting for him only to eat a cold meal.

"Did you find anything?" Annie asked when he started eating.

"No. But I still have several miles of coastline to investigate."

Jack looked at Annie and saw a glassy look in her eyes that told him that Molly had already given his wife her nighttime dose of medicine. That meant she wouldn't be awake much longer.

"How was your day? Did you find one of the books I brought interesting?"

"Yes. I read for several hours this afternoon. Even Molly read for quite a while."

"Good. I'm glad," he said, looking at Molly.

"Are you going to go out again tomorrow?" Annie asked after stifling a yawn.

"Yes. I'm hoping to discover where the smugglers bring their contraband ashore before Quinn and Theo get here."

"Quinn and Theo are coming?"

"Yes, I told you I'd written to them."

"No, you didn't."

"I thought I had," Jack said. He knew it was useless to argue with Annie. She'd no doubt forgotten that he'd written to his friends, but that wasn't unusual for someone taking laudanum.

"No. I wouldn't have forgotten something like that."

"Maybe I didn't, then, Annie. But yes, I wrote them and asked them to help me find the men who are smuggling in opium."

She glared at him, then finished her food. When she was done eating, she drank the rest of her wine, then rose. "I'm tired. I'm going to bed now."

He rose to walk Annie to the room where she'd slept last night. He would love to let her sleep with him in his bed, but he couldn't. He knew they wouldn't just sleep. He knew he would want to hold her. He knew he would want to kiss her. Then they would make love.

Except they wouldn't be making love. They would only be having sex.

"Goodnight, Annie," he said. "I'll no doubt be gone when you wake in the morning," he finished, then left her and Molly and closed the door.

He dressed for bed, then slipped beneath the covers and closed his eyes. But sleep eluded him.

When he thought of what he felt for Annie, his heart swelled inside his chest. He'd loved her more than it was possible for any man to love his wife. And yet…

She wasn't that woman anymore. She'd chosen to leave him. She'd abandoned him because she didn't love him any longer. She'd written him a farewell letter forbidding him from trying to find her. She'd told him she'd rather kill herself than live the rest of her life married to him.

Then she'd let him believe that she had taken her own life. Even though her body had never been found, her shawl and her bonnet were found at the bottom of the cliff. Everyone believed that she'd jumped to her death to avoid a life with him.

No, he could not make love to her until he knew he could forgive her for putting him through two years of hell.

CHAPTER SIX

THE COASTLINE REVEALED itself to be peppered with hundreds of small caves. For five consecutive days Jack searched each of them without any luck. If this stretch of land was where the smugglers brought their contraband ashore, he hadn't found the cave they were using.

Each day he rose early, picked up some pastries for Annie and Molly, then left to search the coastline. Some days Jonah joined him as they went from cave to cave. Other days he searched on his own. He expected Quinn and Theo any day now. Things would go faster once they arrived.

His relationship with Annie wasn't better. In fact, it was getting worse every day.

Jack struggled to figure out why she was so angry with him. Finally, however, he realized that she wasn't angry with him. She was angry at herself. She was angry because she felt guilty. Guilty because she was dependent on a poison that was destroying her, that was destroying their marriage. That was destroying any chance they had of being happy.

But most of all, she hated herself for what she had allowed to happen to her. She hated herself because she was taking a drug that made her feel inferior, made her feel worthless. And she retaliated by taking her frustration and self-loathing out on him.

Jack stopped to eat the bread, cheese, and wine he'd brought with him, then began his search again. This stretch of coastline looked the most promising of any that he'd investigated so far. The caves here were larger than the ones he'd searched earlier, and they were also deeper. It was important to find caves that were deep enough that the smugglers could dig tunnels that would gradually climb to the ground above, and these were perfect. There were also several well-used paths that led from the sea to the caves.

Jack investigated several paths that had obviously been used in the last day or so, then entered one of the largest caves.

Impressions of footprints were still deep in the sand, possibly from the smugglers carrying cases of contraband. This was no doubt one of the caves where the smugglers had hidden cases of opium.

Jack followed the footprints, hoping to find proof that this was where the smugglers had been. He anchored his hand against the wall of the cave, lit the candle he'd brought, then slowly made his way as far as he could. He didn't want to attract any attention in case some of the smugglers were still here. He couldn't risk being discovered.

He took several steps deeper into the cave and saw a dim light shining ahead. Someone was there. He was sure of it. He extinguished the candle and crept through the shadows toward the light. He stopped when he heard voices.

There were at least three smugglers up ahead of him, and Jack pressed his back against the cave wall and listened.

"When will these cases be taken out of here?" the first man said.

"Tonight. The boss is in a hurry to get them moved as soon as possible. He's been in a fierce mood since someone managed to free the girl. I'm not sure what hold he had over her, but he lost his advantage when someone took her. I overheard him say if the authorities get to her, she could take us all down."

"I overheard the boss tell some of the men that she owns the land above us. The boss has tried to force her to give him the deed, but she won't. He even took her baby and refused to give her back until she signs over the land, but that didn't work either."

"No wonder he's as growly as an angry bear."

"Yah, and now he can't find her."

"Somebody has to know where she is."

"He's got people watching every place where they sell laudanum. She won't be able to go very long without it. Either she'll have to surface to buy some, or Molly will. Then we'll catch her."

Jack tipped his head back until it touched the hard rock. He was glad Jonah had volunteered to supply them with more laudanum. If the smugglers were watching for her or Molly to buy laudanum, they'd both be dead if they caught them.

"We're done here," the first smuggler said. "Let's leave before the boss comes to check on us."

Jack turned to leave before he was discovered. He took one step toward the opening of the cave, and his foot kicked a rock, which ricocheted against the wall of the cave with a loud clatter.

"What was that?" one of the smugglers asked.

"Someone's here," another smuggler said, and Jack heard them run toward him.

He knew he was outnumbered, and he didn't have that big of a head start that he could outrun them. He ran to the opening of the cave, but before he made it into the open, someone grabbed him from behind.

Jack turned and hit the first smuggler. The man went down hard and didn't get back up. Jack managed to take another few steps, but the remaining smugglers overpowered him and pulled him to the ground.

Their hold was too great, and he couldn't escape their grasp. He struggled to fight them off, but the third smuggler recovered and punched him in the stomach and the kidneys and jaw while the other two held him.

Jack fought them off as best he could, using his feet to kick out at them, but their hold was too confining.

"Jack! Are you in there?"

The three men holding him stopped. "We gotta get outta here," one of them said. "Someone's coming."

"Let him go," another replied. "He's hurt bad 'nough he'll probably die."

"He'd better, or the boss ain't going to be happy with us," the third said.

"He'll only be mad if he finds out what happened, and I'm not stupid enough to tell him. Are you?"

"Not me," the third smuggler answered. "Let's get out of here."

The smugglers released their hold, and Jack fell to the ground. He struggled with the little strength he had left to stay awake, but his world kept going dark around him.

"Jack!" the voice called out again.

"Jonah," Jack cried out, but his voice was too weak. He doubted the doctor could hear him.

"Jack!"

"Here," he called out a little louder.

A few moments later, Jonah entered the mouth of the cave. "Bloody hell, Jack. What happened?"

"I found where they are...hiding the...opium."

Jonah went to the back of the cave and returned a few minutes later. "There must be at least fifty cases of opium back there."

"That many? Bloody hell."

Jonah wrapped his arm around Jack's shoulders and struggled to get him to his feet. "Come on. I've got to get you back and take care of you."

"Wait," Jack said.

"What for?"

"We have to destroy the opium."

"How?"

"Burn it," Jack growled.

"Yes," Jonah said. "You stay here, Jack, and I'll start a fire."

He helped Jack lean against the wall of the cave, then went to the back and started a fire. Jack drew his pistol and stumbled to a place where he could give Jonah cover. When the blaze was large enough not to go out, Jonah spread the flames to the rest of the cargo.

The crates of opium burned at an alarming rate, and before long, the entire load of contraband was up in flames. Smoke billowed from the burning cargo, and Jonah ran back to Jack and helped him to his feet.

"Don't breathe too deeply or you'll begin to feel the effects of the drug," the doctor warned him.

"I don't have to worry about that. I can barely take in a shallow breath. I think I have some broken ribs."

"Let's get you back to Mrs. Walters' and take care of you." Jonah lent his support as Jack rose gingerly to his feet. "Although," he said as they made their way across the sandy shore, "the smell of opium might help with the pain you're no doubt going to feel."

Jack laughed and immediately clutched his chest. "No more jokes," he gasped. He'd had quite enough pain for one day, thank you very much.

CHAPTER SEVEN

ANNIE PACED THE bedroom again then stopped in front of the window that looked out onto the alley below. No sign of Jack yet.

"Why don't you sit down, mistress, and have a cup of tea. It's still hot."

"I can't, Molly. Where is he? It's been dark for hours. Jack said he'd be back before dinner."

"Maybe he found something he needed to investigate," Molly said.

"Or maybe something happened to him and he can't return."

Annie couldn't explain why she was so worried about Jack. She didn't understand it. It was only hours ago that she was hardly civil to him, and now, when she thought he might be injured—or, heaven forbid, dead—she was terrified she might never see him again.

She tried to tell herself she didn't care for him that much, but that was a lie. She cared for him as much if not more than she'd ever cared for him. She loved him. And she was sure he loved her. Except she couldn't let him. She wasn't worth loving. She wasn't the same person she'd been two years ago. Jack deserved someone better. Much better.

"Why don't you sit down, mistress. You're upsetting yourself."

Annie knew Molly was only attempting to calm her. The young girl was just as worried as she was.

She returned to the window. "I need more of my medicine, Molly."

"No, ma'am. You just had some not that long ago."

"But I need more."

"The doctor wouldn't approve of you having another dose this close to the last one."

"I don't care. I need it."

"Why don't you watch out the window for a bit? I think the major should return any moment now."

Annie went to the window and looked down on the alley below.

"Do you see anything?" Molly asked after a little while.

"No, nothing."

"Just keep watch. I'm sure the major will be back soon."

Annie focused on the alley again, and this time she saw movement. "Here he is, Molly! I see him!"

"I told you he'd be here before long."

"Yes, but…" Her gaze locked on the two men approaching the back door to the lodging house. Dr. Reynolds was with Jack and was holding him up, helping him walk.

"Jack has been hurt," Annie said, rushing to the door.

Molly raced after her. "No, mistress! Don't open the door until they're here. We don't know if they were followed."

Annie placed her hand on the door, ready to turn the lock the second Jack told her to open the door.

"Annie," a voice called out, but it wasn't Jack's deep baritone. It was the doctor, and he sounded worried.

She turned the lock and threw the door open. "Molly, turn back the covers."

Molly took care of the bed while Annie helped Dr. Reynolds assist Jack into the room and place him on the bed.

"What happened, Jack?" she asked while she brought over a basin of water and some clean cloths.

"I ran into some unfriendly fellows," he said, trying to make light of his attack.

Annie rinsed the cloth and washed the cuts on his face. While she did that, Dr. Reynolds removed Jack's shirt and Molly removed his boots. When the shirt fell away, Annie got a look at her husband's torso. His flesh was already starting to bruise, and she could see the boot prints where he'd been kicked.

"From the look of you, I think those fellows were a little more than unfriendly."

"Yes, they might have been," he said, then moaned when Jonah moved him to a sitting position.

The doctor reached in his bag and took out several rolls of bandages, then started wrapping Jack's torso. "This is going to hurt, Jack, but I have to make it tight. It will help you heal faster."

While the doctor worked on Jack, Annie filled a glass with some whiskey and held it to her husband's mouth so he could drink. After he finished, she filled his glass again, but this time just gave him small sips.

"Did you recognize any of the smugglers?" she asked.

"No. But I only saw three of them."

"Did you find where they stored the opium?"

"Yes. They're using a cave at the bottom of the cliff. It's a perfect location for hiding their contraband."

"You would have been proud of your husband," the doctor said. "He drove the smugglers off."

"Actually, your arrival drove them away," Jack said. "I just let them hit me…long enough to wear them out."

Jonah laughed as he finished tying off the strips wrapped around Jack's torso. "But that wasn't the best part," he said when he was finished.

Annie held out a glass of whiskey to the doctor, then gave Jack another swallow of his own. "What was the best part?" she said when the doctor was done and she sat on the bed next to Jack. She reached for his hand and held it. It was important that she touch him. That she kept a part of him close to her.

"The best part was starting the crates of opium ablaze and watching them burn," the doctor said. "You should have seen the flames and the smoke. It was a sight to behold."

Jack looked at her and smiled. "I can assure you that whoever intended to sell the opium won't be pleased when he discovers his cargo is gone. Nor will the buyers."

Annie looked at Molly with an expression of horror.

"What is it, Annie?" Jack asked.

"Nothing," she answered slowly.

"Yes there is. Why do you look like that?"

"Like what?" she said, trying to put a relaxed expression on her face.

"Like you aren't pleased to know we destroyed the opium. Like you know who the leader is and you're afraid of what he'll do when he discovers what happened."

"Don't be silly. Why should I care if you destroyed someone's opium? There's plenty more for sale in the market."

"Yes, there is. But you look as if you know who this shipload of opium belonged to and you're afraid of him."

"Maybe I am," she said. "Maybe I don't know *who* he is, but I know the cargo you destroyed was worth a lot of money, and the smugglers will be looking for you. And they won't be looking for you to thank you for what you did."

"Don't worry, Annie. They won't find me."

"Oh, Jack. You need to stay in hiding. The ringleader isn't going to let what you did go unpunished. He'll be looking for you. You need to hide up here and not leave."

"I'm going to have to for a while," he said. "Until I can move easier."

"How long will it be before Quinn and Theo get here?" she asked.

What Jack said terrified her. If her stepmother's son found Jack before he was completely healed, he didn't stand a chance of defending himself. Annie had never known anyone meaner than Colin. He wouldn't hesitate to kill Jack. Or anyone else who got in his way.

"They should be here any day."

"That won't be soon enough," she said, trying not to sound too terrified. But it was impossible.

"You can't go out either, Annie. I overheard the smugglers say that they're looking for you. They're watching every place that sells laudanum. They think you'll have to buy some soon."

Annie looked at Molly. "That means you'll have to stay here too, Molly. The smugglers who held me captive know you were with me."

Feeling helpless, Annie rose from the bed and paced the floor, thinking of everything that could happen if Colin or his men saw Molly.

Annie stopped, then clasped her hands around her arms and rubbed them. She needed some medicine but didn't want Jack or Dr. Reynolds to know how desperate she was to take it while they were here.

Her skin crawled as if a million spiders crept over her body, and her hands trembled so violently that she knew she couldn't hold anything. Her eyes refused to focus, and she felt as though she was watching what was going on from high above her.

She usually didn't let her craving get this bad. She usually took some of her medicine before she got to this point, but worry over Jack had increased her demand for the laudanum.

She took a cloth that was lying on the table beside the basin and wiped the perspiration from her face. It was suddenly very warm in the room, and the walls seemed to have moved in around her.

She hoped she could last a few more minutes. Surely Dr. Reynolds would go soon. Surely Molly could see that Annie needed her medicine and would give her some.

But it wasn't Molly who walked to the table where the vial of laudanum sat. It was the doctor. He poured wine into a glass and added a few drops of the precious elixir, then brought it to her.

"Here, drink this. Just a sip or two, mind you."

Annie took the glass and tried to bring it to her mouth, but her hands trembled so violently that she couldn't hold it steady enough to drink. To help her, Dr. Reynolds took the glass and held it to her lips.

Annie drank, then paused until that euphoric calm washed over her. She sank down into the chair and waited for her spiked nerves to relax. The sensation was the ultimate feeling of lightness and serenity. She closed her eyes and took several calming breaths.

"Better?" Dr. Reynolds asked.

Annie nodded.

"Your mistress should be all right until morning, Molly. If she wakes you during the night, just give her a small drink of her mixture. But not too much."

"Yes, doctor," Molly answered.

"Annie?" Jack said, concern evident in his voice.

"I'm fine now, Jack."

Jonah filled a glass with whiskey and placed it on the table next to the bed, then walked to the door. "I don't want to risk drawing attention to you by coming to see you for the next day or two, Jack. On my way out, I'll talk to Mrs. Walters to make arrangements for her to provide meals."

Jack grabbed some money from the bedside table and held it out to Jonah. "Give her this and tell her we appreciate her help."

Jonah nodded and took the money. "I'll see you in a few days," he said, then left the room.

"Molly," Jack said when Jonah was gone. "I want you to stay with your mistress tonight."

"I'll be fine, Jack."

He shook his head. "I want someone with you. I won't be able to reach you fast enough should you need anything."

She looked at the concern on Jack's face and experienced a warmth that ran through her veins. Suddenly, scenes of the life she and Jack had shared before Colin destroyed it appeared in her mind, and she remembered how happy they'd been. She remembered how perfect their life had been.

"You can go, Molly. I'll be in shortly," she said.

"Be sure to check that the doors are locked, Molly," Jack added.

"Yes, Major." Molly left the room, and Annie turned to follow her.

"Would you sit with me for a moment, Annie? I'd like to talk to you."

She stopped, then turned and sat in the chair across from Jack's bed. "What would you like to talk about?"

"I think you know, don't you?"

"I suppose I do, but I don't want to talk about that now."

She wrapped her arms around her waist and tried to hold what he wanted to hear inside her. She didn't want him to know what had happened to her. She didn't want to tell him how weak she'd been. She didn't want to see the disappointment on his face when she told him how she'd failed him.

"It's time you told me exactly what happened to you, Annie."

She shook her head. "I can't, Jack. Some of it I don't even remember."

"Then tell me what you do remember." He paused and took in a shallow breath that made him wince. He stifled a groan and held his ribs. "Tell me how you got here," he said in a shaky voice.

"I don't know."

"Why did you write me that letter? Why did you want me to think you had taken your life? At least tell me that much."

Annie bolted from her chair. "I didn't want to write it, Jack. But they made me."

"Who made you?"

"I don't know!" she cried.

"And I think you do, Annie. I think you know exactly who took you and why."

"I don't want to talk about this now. I can't think, and you're confusing me."

"I don't mean to, Annie. I just want to know why you wrote that letter. Why you wrote that you couldn't stand to live with me any longer. Why you wrote that we weren't meant for each other when we were. I wasn't meant to be with anyone other than you. And you were meant to be with me. I want to know why for two years you let me believe you were dead when you weren't. Why you let me die a little every day I thought you were dead."

Annie couldn't stop the tears from streaming down her face. She knew the words she wrote him would tear him apart, but at the time she thought letting him believe she was dead was best.

"How did you find out I was still alive?" she asked through her tears.

"I received a note telling me."

"From whom?"

"It wasn't signed."

"But you had to have an idea who had sent it."

"I do. I assume it was Molly, but she only wrote it because she's a very loyal friend to you, and she feared for you. She didn't want you to die, and they were going to kill you."

She closed her eyes and recalled the days before Jack came for her. She had been close to death. She knew she had. She was only alive now because Molly had written the note to tell Jack she was still alive.

A painful ache intensified in Annie's chest, tightening around her heart. She couldn't face Jack after all she'd done to him.

She turned and took a step to leave him.

"Will you answer at least one question before you leave?"

Annie stopped. "Only one, Jack. I owe you that much."

"Why do you want me to believe that you don't love me when I know you do?"

She slowly turned until her gaze locked with Jack's. Tears still streamed down her cheeks, and the pain inside her breast grew more intense. "Because I'm not the same person I was two years ago. You may think you love me, but you can't. I'm not worth loving. Too much has happened, and it's not possible to undo any of it."

"Like what, Annie? What can't you undo?"

"What I've become, Jack. The day will come when you'll expect me to choose between you and my medicine, and you won't like the choice I make."

The look on Jack's face tore at her insides. She knew that would be his reaction. She knew he couldn't believe she would actually say that and mean it. But she did. She could never give up her medicine. She'd tried once and would never go through that pain again.

"I'm tired. I need to go to bed." She turned, then walked to the door that would take her to the next room.

"Goodnight, Jack."

Chapter Eight

J ACK STAYED AWAKE almost all night, partly because he was in so
much physical pain from the beating he'd taken it was
impossible to get to sleep, and partly because he couldn't stop
thinking of his conversation with Annie. She'd coldly told him
there was no hope for them. She'd told him that if she had to
choose between the opium she was dependent on and their
marriage, she would choose the opium.

Was that why she'd let him believe she was dead? So he
wouldn't come after her and discover what she had become?

Jack closed his eyes and took a deep breath. Something more
had to have happened to make her believe he would hate her if he
discovered what she had become. Something so threatening that
she'd done the impossible. For two years, she'd allowed him to
believe that she was dead.

He would never understand what had caused her to feign her
death until he knew everything she was keeping from him. Only
then would he be able to have a conversation with his wife and
force her to tell him what he needed to know.

From his bed, Jack stared out the window, watching for the
sun to come up over the horizon.

As dawn began to lighten the sky, the door opened and she
entered his room.

"Good morning," she said.

"Good morning." Jack looked into Annie's eyes and knew at a glance that she'd already had her morning laudanum. It was amazing how clearly he could tell if she was under the influence of opium, or if she was craving the opiate to calm her nerves.

"Can I get you anything?" she asked.

"Would you help me sit?"

"Are you sure you're well enough to get up?"

"It won't hurt any more to sit than it does to lie here," Jack said with a grimace as he pulled back the covers.

Annie assisted him to the chair, then covered him with a blanket from the bed. When he was settled, there was a knock on the door, and she went to open it.

"Good morning, Mrs. Walters," Annie said, though no smile lightened her face.

"I brought your breakfast. There are even some pastries from the bakery. Dr. Reynolds said you were partial to sticky buns," Mrs. Walters said, then placed the tray on the corner of the desk near the window.

"Yes. Thank you," Annie replied.

Jack heard none of his wife's former kindness in her tone. Her words were simply appropriate, but without warmth. The pain he felt at the realization was nearly unbearable.

"Thank you, Mrs. Walters," Jack said. "I can't tell you how grateful we are for everything you've done for us."

"I don't mind," Mrs. Walters said, then paused long enough to pour Annie and Jack cups of tea. "I'll have a hearty stew for your lunch," the landlady said on her way out of the room.

The door closed softly, and suddenly he and Annie were alone.

She handed Jack his cup of tea and a sticky bun, then sat down in front of him with her own. They ate in silence while Jack decided how to begin the conversation he knew they had to have.

When they'd finished, he put his cup down. "We need to talk, Annie. We need to finish our conversation from last night."

She lowered her gaze and stared at her hands locked in her

lap. "I don't want to, Jack."

"I know you don't, but we have to get everything out into the open. We can't go on until we do." He shifted in his chair so he could look into Annie's eyes. "When I confronted the smugglers yesterday in the cave, they said something about a parcel of land. They mentioned that it was land that you owned. What is that all about?"

"They said that?"

"Yes. I wasn't aware that you held the title to a piece of land. Where is this land?"

He watched her eyes, wary that she was going to avoid being honest. Annie, in turn, seemed to study him. Her eyes pierced him with a momentary defiance, and then subtly changed. With a long, slow sigh, she began to speak.

"It's the stretch of land above the caves where the smugglers hide their contraband. My father owned it, and he willed it to me when he died."

"Why does the man who is smuggling in opium want this land?"

"Because in the back of the cave where they store the opium, there's a path that leads above ground. The tunnel opens in back of a building the smugglers want to use to hide the opium until they take it to London. I own the ground and the building."

"Annie, do you know who the leader of this smuggling gang is?"

Her eyes lowered sharply, and Jack realized she did.

"Who is he? What's his name? How do you know him?"

"Don't, Jack. I don't want to talk about him."

"Who is he, Annie? How did you get messed up with him?"

A hundred different answers swirled in his mind. He could easily imagine a dozen terrible things that might have happened to his wife while he was away on the queen's assignment.

"Who is he, Annie? What's his name?"

"Jack, don't."

"Who, Annie!"

She gasped, and a hand flew to cover her mouth with trembling fingers.

"Colin."

"Colin who?"

"Graves. Colin Graves."

"How do you know this Colin Graves?"

"He's my stepmother's son."

Jack stared at Annie for a long moment without speaking. "Start from the beginning, Annie," he said slowly, "and don't leave anything out."

"I can't, Jack."

"You can, Annie. You have to."

She took in a deep breath that trembled when she released it. "You know my father remarried after Mother died."

Jack nodded.

"My stepmother has a son from her first marriage. His name is Colin Graves. He was always in trouble with the authorities and always coming to Father for money. Finally, Father refused to give him any more, and even refused to let him step on our property."

Annie lowered her gaze, and Jack realized that she was afraid of the man.

"Father especially forbade him to be anywhere near me. I was glad. I was terrified of him. He was mean and he frightened me. But when my father died, he started coming around all the time.

"He always had a plan or a scheme he was involved in. He always needed money, and his mother gave it to him. I never knew what schemes he was involved in, but I knew they weren't legal.

"Then I met you and fell in love. We married, and you took me to Burnhaven. I didn't think I'd ever have to see Colin again."

"But he came while I was gone," Jack said.

"Yes," Annie whispered. "When you were away on that last assignment, Colin came to Burnhaven. He demanded I hand over the deed to the land that my father left me. It had been in Father's family for generations. It had been used by smugglers more than a hundred years ago. Father made me promise to never sell it. He was afraid it would be used by smugglers again."

"Which is why Colin wanted it."

"Yes," she said softly. "There's a path that leads from the sea to one of the caves then to a tunnel that slopes up to the cliff, then to the mansion at the top of the ridge. From there, you could load the contraband onto wagons and deliver the smuggled goods directly to London."

"No wonder Colin wants the land so badly."

"I refused to let him have it as long as I could, but I wasn't strong enough to fight him."

"And I wasn't there to protect you."

She lowered her gaze to her hands still clenched in her lap.

"Go on, Annie. Then what happened?"

She swiped at a tear that spilled down her cheek. "One day, Colin came with some men. They gave me one last chance to hand over the deed to the land. I had hidden it well and refused to give it to him, so they kidnapped me.

"I don't think Colin expected me to keep the deed to the land hidden from him as long as I did, but I proved more determined than he thought I'd be. I couldn't give it to him, Jack. I'd promised Father I'd never let anyone have the land."

Jack reached for her hand and held it. "What happened isn't your fault, Annie. If it's anyone's fault, it's mine."

"Colin knew he had to get the deed before you found out that he'd taken me. He was afraid of you. Afraid that you'd tell the authorities what he was doing and he'd go to prison. Or hang. So he decided to weaken me by giving me doses of laudanum. I know he would have killed me if he found the deed, but I had hidden it too well."

"And you still have it?" Jack asked.

"I should think so. I buried it where no one would think to look."

"Good."

"He gave me more and more laudanum. I fought it, Jack. I begged him to stop. And then…then I just begged him to give me more. I was rarely lucid. I suppose he thought that would make me tell him where the deed was." She laughed sadly. "And I would have. I know I would have. But most days I couldn't even remember where I'd buried it."

"Could you find it now?"

"Yes."

Jack wanted very much to reach out and pull Annie onto his lap and hold her, but he sensed by her stiffness that she wasn't ready. It was obvious she didn't trust him, and he knew why. She was still dependent on laudanum, and more than anything, she feared he would take it away from her. She'd already suffered so much, and giving up her laudanum was the last thing she could handle.

"Then you started searching for me, Jack. Or at least in my nightmares you did. And then I overheard them say you'd come to Burnhaven. That you were getting too close. That's when Colin forced me to write the letter telling you that I didn't love you any longer." Her voice trailed away to a whisper. "And couldn't stand to be your wife."

Annie lifted her gaze and looked at Jack. He tried to keep the pain from his eyes but couldn't. Her words in the letter had hurt him. But now he knew they were intended to hurt him so badly that he would stop looking for her.

"I knew you'd be hurt by what I wrote, but I couldn't afford to care. I knew if you kept searching for me, Colin would kill you."

"But I didn't stop searching for you, Annie. I couldn't."

"That's why I faked my death. I needed you to believe I was dead. You had to be convinced so you would stop looking for me, or Colin would have killed you."

Jack lowered his head to his hands. His breathing was harsh and labored. Thankfully, Annie gave him time to accustom himself to what she'd told him. Then she continued.

"Colin was losing patience with me. He demanded that I give him the deed, or he was going to kill me and keep searching for the deed until he found it, which he never would have done. But I got sick. I threw up each and every day, and I think that was the first time Colin realized I might actually die and he'd never find the deed. He stopped giving me any more medicine, and one day, Molly came to take care of me."

"Didn't he get a doctor for you?"

She laughed, a sound that carried an odd note of melancholy. "There was no need."

"But—"

"No need, Jack. It's when I discovered that I was pregnant."

ANNIE SMILED. "IT took me a while to figure it out, but when I did, I couldn't stop crying. I didn't know if I was crying because I was happy I was going to have our baby, or if I was crying because I was terrified to bring a child into such a dreadful situation."

She rose from her chair and walked to the window, then looked out onto the alley below for several long minutes. "Those were the most beautiful, terrifying months of my life," she said, then turned to face him.

She needed him to understand that she could never be the wife he wanted her to be. That they could never share the love they'd once had for each other.

"I can't give up my medicine," Annie said. "I need it too much, Jack. Colin forced me to give it up when he realized I was pregnant, and I can't go through that hell again. I'm not strong enough."

"But you are, Annie. Jonah and I would be there with you."

"No! I know what it was like before, and I won't do it again."

Jack didn't say anything for a few moments. "What happened then?"

"Colin sent me to live at Radbury House, that horrid asylum. That's where Lillie was born."

"I'm so sorry, Annie," he said softly, and she knew he was sorry for everything she'd gone through. He was sorry that he hadn't been there to help her. That he hadn't been there when his daughter was born.

"And then?"

"Before I had time to even get to know our baby, someone stole her. I don't know where they took her, or who took care of her. I don't even know if she's still alive or if Colin had her killed. I have to believe, since he took care of me the entire time I was carrying her, he didn't kill her. I'm sure she's still alive, Jack. That belief is all that has kept me going since they took her."

Annie turned away. "I think I went a little crazy then. I wanted to see my baby, but they wouldn't let me. I just wanted to make sure she was all right, that she was safe, but they refused to let me see her. I screamed and scratched and bit anyone who came near me. That's when they started giving me medicine again. More than before. Sometimes so much I didn't know who I was or what was happening around me."

Jack reached out to hold her hand, but she pulled away from him. She couldn't rely on him. She couldn't give in to him. It would make her weak, and she had to stay strong. For her own sake.

"Stay with me, Annie. I'm hurting too. I want to find our daughter and make sure she's safe. Won't you let me help you?"

"You can't," she answered with tears running down her face. Didn't he know she wasn't worth being loved by him? Didn't he know that she would never be the wife he wanted and needed? And deserved?

She'd gone through a time when the drug she was so dependent on had been taken away from her, and she'd never endure that torture again. She wasn't strong enough to endure it a second time. She couldn't do it. Not even for him.

Annie got to her feet. "Enough," she said. "We've talked

enough for today."

She turned to walk to her room. Before she could leave Jack, there was a knock on the door, and she moved to answer it.

"Wait, Annie."

She paused, startled by the commanding tone in his voice. Jack signaled her to be silent, then took his gun from the drawer on the bedside table. When he had it cocked and aimed, he nodded for her to open the door.

She turned the doorknob and stepped back, pressing her back against the wall behind the door.

"That's a hell of a way to greet your friends," Quinn said as he and Theo entered the room.

Chapter Nine

Jack took a deep breath then released the hammer on the gun pointed at his two fellow agents. "Come in," he said, and put the gun back on the bedside table.

"How are you?" Quinn looked at Jack, then frowned. "You look as if you were run over by a barrel wagon."

"I had a discussion with our smugglers, and they took exception to my questions."

"Well, you look like hell," Theo said, then he and Quinn took a seat in the two empty chairs that sat nearby.

"I've been waiting for you." Jack looked at his wife. "Would you offer our guests a drink, Annie?"

Annie walked to the liquor bottles on the table and poured Quinn and Theo each a glass of brandy, then sat on the edge of the bed.

"Hello, Annie," Theo greeted her. "It's been a long time since we've seen you."

"Yes, it has. Jack tells me you've both married since we last saw each other."

"Yes," Quinn said with a smile. "You and Jack should pay us a visit. But don't plan on getting a lot of rest when you come. It's not too quiet at Rosemont with five small children."

"Five?" Annie asked.

"I didn't tell you about Quinn's family," Jack said. "He was left with his brother's two daughters when his brother and sister-in-law died."

"Oh, I'm sorry," she said.

"Thank you," Quinn replied.

"Then his wife presented him with triplets."

"Triplets?"

"Yes," Quinn answered, and Jack could see the pride on his face. "Three very active boys. They keep us all very busy, day and night."

"Oh my," Annie said. "Do they all look alike?"

"Don't tell anyone, but there are times when I can't tell them apart."

"What about your wife? Does she have trouble telling them apart?"

"No. She could tell them apart from the very beginning. She says all mothers can tell their children apart, no matter how much they resemble each other."

"Yes," she said, though she seemed lost in thought. "A mother would know."

Jack watched the polite smile leave Annie's face. He knew she'd had the same thought he'd just been struck with. If they were lucky enough to find her, would either of them know their own child?

"So, fill us in on what's going on here," Theo said to fill the awkward silence.

Annie stood, then turned to face Jack. "I know you and your friends have a great deal to discuss, and I'm getting tired, so I think I'll go to my room."

"Will you be all right, Annie?" he asked.

"Fine, Jack. Molly is probably waiting. She'll take care of me."

"Yes. No doubt. Rest well," he said, then watched Annie until she left the room.

When they were alone, Jack looked at his friends. "Lock the door, will you, Theo."

Theo rose and locked the door, then returned to his chair.

"All right, Jack. Out with it. It's time we heard the entire story."

"And don't leave anything out," Quinn added. "It's obvious that what is going on involves Annie."

"There's a full bottle of brandy on the table. Refill our glasses, will you, Theo?"

"Are you saying we're going to need it?" Theo asked.

"That's exactly what I'm saying."

Theo refilled their glasses, then sat down to listen to what Jack had to say.

"There's a great deal I don't understand yet, but I'll let you know what I know. You're correct about Annie. Two years ago, when I was on assignment, she was kidnapped."

"Kidnapped!" Theo said. "By whom?"

"By a man called Colin Graves. He's the son of Annie's step-mother by her first husband."

"What could they possibly want with Annie?" Quinn asked.

"Annie's father owned a prime strip of land along the coast. Prime because it was a perfectly located piece of land with several caves large enough for smugglers to unload their boats and hide their shipments of opium. Annie's father willed her the land on the condition that she would never sell it.

"Colin Graves is the leader of this band of smugglers, and he's determined to own the land. He wanted Annie to sign the deed over to him. But she refused."

"That was a brave decision," Theo said. "Whoever owns the land can charge a hefty price to other smugglers as well."

"A perfect location for Graves to unload his opium, then smuggle it into London where he can sell it without having to pay taxes on it," Quinn surmised.

"I'm sure that's what he's been doing," Jack said.

"Which the authorities aren't looking favorably upon."

"No. That was why I was sent here, to discover what I could about this smuggling ring and bring it down."

"Have you found this cave?"

"Yes. But it gets worse." Jack took a swallow from his glass.

"After Annie was kidnapped and brought here, she realized she was pregnant. I have a daughter. She's a little over a year old."

"Where is she?" Quinn asked.

"Annie doesn't know. Graves took the baby shortly after she was born, and we don't know where she is."

"Damn him," Theo said. "I hope you let me kill him."

"No, Theo. He's mine. When he dies, it will be by my hand," Jack said, then took another swallow from his glass. "And there's more."

His friends sat in silence, and Jack continued. "Annie wasn't a very cooperative captive. She tried to escape several times and caused the guards and everyone else a lot of trouble. To keep her calm, she was given doses of laudanum. It made her more cooperative and compliant. They needed her to sign the deed over to Graves and used the laudanum to make her submissive."

"How long has she been taking the laudanum?" Quinn asked.

"Steadily since our daughter was born. And the more trouble she caused, the more laudanum they forced down her."

"I'm sorry, Jack, but you're going to have to fight me for the pleasure of ridding the world of this monster," Quinn said. "He deserves a special kind of death, and I'm an expert in the art of torture."

"No, Quinn. He's mine," Jack repeated.

"What about your daughter?" Quinn asked. "Do you have any idea where she is?"

Jack raked his hand down his face. "I don't even know if she's alive. I pray she is. I'm not sure how Annie will take it if they've killed her."

"It's one thing to poison an adult with drugs, but to kill a baby?" Quinn growled. "It takes a special kind of monster to do that."

"I pray Graves isn't that demented."

"I think he knows that if he harms your babe, your wife will never sign over the land he's so desperate to have."

Jack nodded. "I keep telling myself that."

"So," Theo said, placing his glass on the table. "What are your plans?"

"Graves may well be the leader of this group of smugglers, but there's someone else. Someone Graves answers to."

"What makes you think that?"

"From what Annie says, he doesn't have the intelligence to organize an operation like this. Nor the influence to find buyers for the opium. He's a petty thief with a reputation for being in and out of trouble. And he spends nearly all his time here. The mastermind behind this operation has to have strong ties in London. That's no doubt where his sales are made."

"Do you know who he is?" Theo asked.

Jack shook his head. "Hopefully, we can take Graves alive and make him talk."

"So, how are we going to get our hands on Graves?" Quinn asked.

"We're going to keep watch for the next shipment to arrive. When it does, we're going to attack. We're going to take down the smugglers and capture Colin Graves. Then we're going to find my daughter." Jack struggled a moment with unexpected emotion before he squared his shoulders and continued. "How many men did you bring with you?"

"Twenty," Quinn replied.

"Good. Take them with you to the inn down the street and feed them, then get them settled. We'll leave around two o'clock and I'll show you where the smugglers come ashore. We'll post a watch there."

"Are you well enough to stay awake all night?" Quinn said. "Maybe you should—"

"I'll sleep tomorrow," Jack said.

"We should have known that," Theo said with a grin.

"Get some rest now," Jack said as Theo and Quinn walked to the door. "Oh, one more thing," Jack said, stopping them before they left the room. "Would you go to the infirmary and tell Dr. Reynolds our plan? It's across the street from the bakery."

"Does he know what's going on?" Theo asked.

"Yes. He's the one who saved me from the smugglers, or I wouldn't be standing here talking to you."

"We'll let him know," Quinn said. "In fact, we'll be glad to have him along."

"He'll be an asset to us. He wants to be involved in taking down this ring of smugglers. He's the one who has to treat anyone with a dependence on the drug. He deserves to be in on the capture of the ring."

Quinn and Theo nodded, then left.

Jack finished the brandy in his glass, then lowered his head against the back of the chair. He thought of what he wanted to accomplish tomorrow, or the next day, or the one after that. He wanted to eliminate the smuggling ring and shut off the supply of opium. He wanted to keep the drug out of the hands of more innocent victims like Annie. He wanted to prevent the band of smugglers from ruining any more lives.

And he wanted to find his daughter.

He poured a small amount of brandy into his glass and brought it to his mouth, then hesitated when the door to Annie's room opened and she entered. She sat in a chair opposite him.

"Quinn and Theo have left, then."

"Yes. They're going to get some rest, then meet back here around two."

"And then what, Jack?"

"We're going to stop them, Annie. We're going to catch them when they bring the contraband ashore and arrest Colin and the rest of the smugglers."

"What will happen to Colin?"

"The authorities will lock him away so he can't hurt anyone else like he did you. Or…maybe he'll hang. Then we're going to find our daughter and take her to Burnhaven."

"What about me?" she asked.

"What do you mean?"

"How long will you allow me to have my medicine?"

She tried to hide the terrified look on her face, but Jack saw it. He recognized the fear in her eyes. "The day will come, Annie, when you won't need your medicine anymore. Jonah said he'd help you. And I'll be with you. It won't be easy, but we'll help you get rid of the poison in your body so you won't ever need another dose."

Annie rose from her chair and walked to the only window in the room. She stared out into the darkness for several long minutes. There was nothing to see, but she absently watched as if she was imagining a life without opium playing out in the blackness before her.

"It won't be easy, Annie. I know how difficult it will be, but I'll be with you every step of the way. And it will be worth it. You won't live in an opium-induced haze anymore. You'll be able to watch our little girl grow and remember her taking her first step, and saying her first words. And all the other firsts in her life."

"I can remember those things now, Jack. I'm not as lost as you think I am. I don't *need* my medicine. I can give it up any time I want to."

"But you can't, Annie. If you could, you would have."

She paced the floor, wrapping her arms around her waist as if she was in pain. Tears filled her eyes and spilled over her lashes. "Why are you doing this to me?" she said in an accusing tone.

She was losing control. Jack could see she was. She needed more laudanum to calm her, but she'd just had some not that long ago. The frequency with which she required more was increasing.

He struggled to stand and attempted to gather her in his arms, but she pushed him away.

"Leave me alone! Don't touch me! You don't want to help me. You only want to make me suffer. You're embarrassed by me. You don't want to admit that your wife is dependent on...on..."

"Annie, listen to yourself. Listen to what you're saying."

"I know what I'm saying! You're the one who doesn't understand what I'm saying. You're the one who's ashamed of me. You're the one who thinks I'm worse than I am."

Jack knew it was useless to argue with her. The fear that he would take her opium-laced elixir away from her terrified her. That only proved how dependent she was.

He walked to the place where he'd hidden the vials that Jonah had given him and poured a few drops into a glass of wine. "Here, drink this."

With trembling hands, she took the mixture and drank a large swallow. The exultant expression he saw on her face while she waited for the euphoria the opium would give her terrified him. She was much more dependent than he'd thought she was.

"Go to bed, Annie. You should sleep through the night now."

She sat back down in her chair for a few minutes, then looked up at him. Her glassy gaze told him that the medicine was already working. She was under its influence.

He opened the door to the connecting room. "Molly, your mistress is ready to go to bed. Would you help her, please?"

"Yes, Major."

Molly helped Annie to her room and closed the door behind her.

Jack sank into his chair and buried his head in his hands. He was more terrified for Annie than before. For the first time, he wasn't sure he could help her. He wasn't sure he was strong enough to watch her suffer through what he knew she'd have to endure to get rid of the poison that was in her body. For the first time, he was afraid he would fail her.

And himself.

Tears spilled from his eyes and ran down his cheeks. He hadn't cried this much since his mother died when he was eight years old. But the pain he was experiencing right now was as devastating as the grief he'd realized that horrid night.

Annie lay in bed and replayed every word of their conversation. *The day will come, Annie, when you won't need your medicine anymore.*

Jack was going to take away her medicine, and she knew what that would entail. Her skin would crawl, the nightmares would begin, the voices in her head would swallow her brain. And the rest would follow—the violent tremors, the freezing cold, the burning hot, the gripping pain, the insects that would crawl on every surface she touched. She'd gone through that before when Colin discovered she was pregnant and stopped giving her laudanum.

She knew she could never go through that hell again.

She wouldn't do it. She'd rather die.

She rose from the bed and paced the room. Thankfully, Molly was fast asleep.

Maybe when Jack realized how horrible it would be for her to go through that process, he wouldn't force her to endure such torture. But she knew he would. He wanted her to be like she'd been before. He didn't want a wife who was dependent on a drug. She would be an embarrassment to him. An embarrassment he wouldn't want his friends to be around.

She paced back and forth across the room. She couldn't go through that again. She had to escape him before he forced her to give up her medicine entirely.

She knew what that would entail, and she couldn't do it again. She'd rather live her life alone than endure the agony. She'd rather live without Jack and her baby than have to suffer like that.

Annie packed her few clothes in a bag, then went to where she'd seen Molly hide a bottle of laudanum before she'd left the room. She waited until she heard Jack leave at two o'clock with Quinn and Theo, then she went into his room and took the vials of laudanum he thought he'd hidden so well.

When all was quiet, she went down the stairs and made it out of the house without anyone seeing her. Once she was outdoors, she ran.

She didn't know where she was going—she only knew it had to be far away from Jack. He'd be much better off without her. If she was lucky, he'd realize the same thing and wouldn't come after her.

The only regret she'd have was forsaking her baby. She'd be leaving her child behind and would never see her again.

It was too cruel, but it was the only way. Annie wiped the tears from her face and did the only thing left to her. She ran.

CHAPTER TEN

JACK FELT LIKE hell. Every muscle in his body ached from the beating he'd taken, and crouching behind a rock all night while they kept watch for the smugglers to arrive didn't help. It was daylight now, and he could finally return to Whitstable. He couldn't wait to stretch out in bed. He swore he wouldn't move for at least twelve hours.

It was unlikely that they'd catch the smugglers the first night they watched. Jack had known that. But it had presumably been several days since they'd brought in their last shipment, and he knew it was likely that the next load of opium wouldn't be long in coming.

"I ordered six men to stay here and keep watch for any activity," Quinn said as they mounted their horses and began the trip back to the boarding house.

Jack didn't anticipate that Annie would have any trouble, but for some reason he couldn't explain, he'd been uneasy about leaving her for so many hours. It wasn't that he didn't trust her, but after their conversation yesterday, he felt apprehensive about not being there to watch over her.

He struggled to keep up with Quinn and Theo while replaying her words from the night before. *Leave me alone! Don't touch me! You don't want to help me. You only want to make me suffer.*

Was that really what she thought? Did she really think he

only wanted to make her suffer?

A blanket of fear wrapped around him. What if her terror over stopping her medicine was more powerful than the prospect of being completely free of her dependence on it? What if she would do anything to avoid going through what it would take to rid herself of the poison in her body? And worse, what if she no longer loved him enough to even try?

Jack pushed Comet to go faster.

"Is something wrong, Jack?" Quinn yelled when Jack passed him.

"I need to get to Annie," he bellowed. "I need to make sure she's all right."

Jack went even faster, with Quinn and Theo keeping up with him. When he reached the boarding house he dismounted, then took the stairs as fast as his painful ribs would allow.

When he reached the upper floor where their rooms were located, he saw Molly standing at the top of the stairs. Her eyes were wide with fear and tears streamed down her face.

"Where is she, Molly?"

"She's gone, Major. She left sometime during the night, and I don't know where she went."

Jack ran into the room and searched for any clue as to where she might have gone, then crossed to where he'd hidden the bottles of laudanum Jonah had brought him. They were gone. And it was his fault. He hadn't been careful enough to keep the vials out of her sight, and now she had it all.

"Do you know where she might have gone?" Theo asked when he came into the room.

Jack shook his head. "No, but she's on foot."

"All right," Quinn said. "We'll begin our search on the main street. Maybe someone saw her. If we can find out which direction she went, we'll have a general idea of where she's headed."

Jack nodded, then left the room to begin his search. His friends followed.

They stopped at every shop that was open and asked if they'd seen Annie. Unfortunately, no one had until they reached the bakery.

"Good morning, sir," the lady behind the counter greeted him. "I'm afraid you're a mite early. The sticky buns aren't baked yet."

"I haven't come for pastries this morning. I'm just curious if you sold all your sticky buns from yesterday."

"Just so happens I did. A young woman with blonde hair came in the middle of the night and pounded on the door. She took all the sticky buns I had left from the day before and said you'd come by this morning to pay for the lot. I thought it wasn't safe for her to be out at that time of the night, but she didn't seem to mind."

"What time was this?" Jack asked. It was Annie. There was no doubt.

"Must have been around three in the morning. I always start baking about half past two, and she came in a little after I got here."

Annie must have waited until he left. "Did you see what direction she went?" he asked.

"Oh yes," the lady said. "She went west. Toward Rochester. I suppose she must be on her way to London."

"Thank you," Jack said, then left the shop. "She's headed to London," he told Quinn and Theo. He mounted Comet and urged him to a gallop. Annie had a good four-hour head start, but she was on foot, so they should be able to catch up with her before she got very far.

Jack led the way down the road until he saw a figure walking in the distance. It was a woman, and he was sure it was Annie.

"Wait for me here," he said to his friends, and he rode ahead.

He knew it wasn't possible to surprise her. Annie would hear him coming up behind her, and when she turned, she'd see him and most likely run.

Which was exactly what she did.

He took chase at a gallop and closed the distance between them in seconds.

"Stop, Annie. You can't outrun me."

He was sure she'd continue to run, even though she knew she couldn't get away from him, but she surprised him and stopped.

"Leave me alone, Jack," she cried.

He dismounted and walked to her. He didn't know how much of the opiate she'd taken already, but her eyes were glassy and her gait was unsteady.

"Where are you going?" he asked her.

"Away."

"Why?"

"Why? You want to know why?"

"Yes, Annie. Why do you want to run away from me?"

"I'm trying to save myself, Jack. I know what you intend to do to me, and I can't let you."

Her words were slurred and her voice was strident and shrill.

"What do you think I intend to do to you?"

"You're going to take away my medicine. You're going to force me to stop taking it!"

"And you don't want to?"

"No! I don't want to!"

"Why?"

"I know what it's like to have it taken away! Colin took it away from me when he found out I was pregnant. I got so sick I nearly died."

A heavy weight pressed against his chest. He was right when he'd guessed that Annie didn't think she could give up her medicine. He was right in believing she'd rather live under the influence of opium than go through a short period of agony to rid her body of the poison inside her.

"What if I promise that I won't take it away from you?"

"You'll let me keep taking it?"

"I will."

Jack knew what he was promising her. He didn't know what

living with someone under the influence of opium would be like. It would undoubtedly be a living hell. Yet what choice did he have?

It was his fault she was dependent on opium. If he hadn't left her alone, if he had been with her to protect her, Colin would never have kidnapped her.

Everything Annie had gone through, and everything she was, was his fault. He was responsible for what had happened to her, and he had to take care of her.

"Do you promise?" she asked tentatively.

"I promise, Annie. I promised I would always take care of you. And I will."

She took a step forward until she was in his arms. It was the first time she'd let him hold her. The first time she'd shown a hint of the affection they'd had for each other.

He wrapped his arms around her and gathered her to him.

"I love you, Jack," she whispered. "I dreamt of you every night I was being held in those awful places. I waited for you to come for me. I knew you would."

"I'm sorry it took me so long."

"It's all right now. You're here."

"Yes, I'm here."

"Please, don't leave me."

"I won't, Annie. I'll never leave you again."

She lifted her chin and looked at him with all the love he'd seen in her gaze before any of this happened.

Jack lowered his head and covered her mouth. The kiss they shared was all-consuming. He kissed her again, then deepened it and tried to pretend that nothing had changed between them. But it had. He knew it had. He would just have to convince himself that he would be able to adjust to this new life.

That he could accept this new Annie.

JACK REFUSED TO let Annie out of his sight. Their daily routine became one of watching the shore by night and sleeping by day. Even when they weren't guarding the entrance to the cave, Jack posted guards on the shore to watch for the smugglers. He wasn't going to take even the slightest chance that any would come ashore and be missed.

Tonight was the fourth night Jack, Quinn, Theo, and Jonah watched the shoreline. It was the fourth night they'd watched for smuggled crates of opium to come ashore. It was the fourth night Jack had kept Annie within arm's reach.

"If anything happens tonight, you will stay right here, Annie," he said for at least the tenth time tonight. "I don't want to have to worry about you. I want you to stay hidden behind these rocks and not show your face."

"Don't worry, Jack. I just want to see Colin captured. That's all I want."

He shook his head. He didn't want her to be anywhere near Colin Graves or any of his men, but she hadn't given him a choice. He either brought her with him or she would run away again. Her greatest fear was that if she stayed with him, he would stop giving her the laudanum her body required.

"If they're going to show up," Quinn said, "they'd better do it soon, or they're going to lose the tide."

"They're coming," Theo said, pointing out to sea.

Peering into the black, moonless void, Jack watched as several small boats came ashore. They were low in the water, which meant they were loaded with cargo.

"Do you recognize Graves?" Jack whispered to Annie. "He should be in the first or second boat if he's going to be here."

"I can't tell," Annie said, focusing on the men rowing ashore.

She watched a few more seconds, then placed her hand on Jack's arm. "He's in the first boat. He's at the very front."

"Do your men know what to do?" Jack asked Quinn.

"Yes. They'll wait until the cargo is brought ashore and un-loaded, then take Graves' men as they leave the cave."

Jack nodded.

"Everyone, stay out of sight," Theo whispered, and everyone hunched further down behind the rocks, making sure they were hidden from view.

The boats came ashore, then the smugglers started unloading their cargo. There were five boats, ten smugglers, and the apparent leader of the smuggling ring—Colin Graves. The man who'd ruined Annie's life. And Jack's.

There were more cases of opium than there'd been when Jonah set the previous shipment ablaze.

Jack's heart pounded harder in his chest. If everything went as planned, this would all be over tonight. His assignment would be complete and he could take Annie and his baby home to Burnhaven. He could live the life he'd always dreamed he'd have.

He stared at the one man who didn't lift a finger to help unload the cases of opium. The man who'd caused so much death and destruction. Colin Graves stood at the mouth of the cave and kept watch.

Jack reached for his gun. No matter what, Graves would be arrested, or he would die. He'd pay for what he'd done to her. He'd pay for taking their baby from Annie.

Finally, the last crate of cargo was unloaded. Only then did Graves follow the last crate of opium into the cave.

Theo motioned for the twenty soldiers to get into position, and they moved from where they'd been hiding behind the rocks that surrounded the mouth of the cave. Then they waited.

At last, the smugglers exited the cave. One by one they trudged down the path toward their waiting boats.

The soldiers waited until all were out of the cave, then Quinn gave the signal, and the men surrounded the smugglers and captured them all without firing a shot.

The only smuggler who wasn't in the group was Graves. He was still in the cave.

"Is there another exit to the cave?" Quinn whispered.

"There has to be," Jack answered. "There has to be a way to

get the opium out."

He considered his options. He had to go after Graves or the man would get away. So he readied his pistol and ran into the cave.

"Theo, take care of the smugglers, and make them tell you where the baby is," Quinn yelled, then followed Jack.

Thankfully, torches were still lit, so he could see what was ahead of him, but by the time Jack reached the crates of stacked opium, Graves was nowhere in sight.

"Which way?" Quinn asked when he caught up to Jack.

"We have two choices. The tunnel on the right or the one on the left."

"I'll go right," Quinn said.

"Left it is," Jack said, and grabbed a torch, then plunged into the dark tunnel.

He prayed Graves had gone down this shaft of the cave. The bastard wouldn't give up without a fight, and whoever caught up with him would have to kill him. Jack hoped it was him. If he couldn't take Graves alive, he wanted the pleasure of killing the man himself.

He ran farther into the cave that gradually slanted upward, like a gentle hill. Stealthily, he followed the tunnel, taking care at every turn. Finally, the air seemed lighter and the opening in front of him wasn't as dark.

Jack ran faster. He needed to catch up with Graves before the man reached the opening. Once there, he probably had a horse waiting for him. If he reached his horse, he'd get away. Jack would never catch up with him.

Something told him that Graves was close, that the man who'd ruined Annie's life and stolen his baby daughter was within reach. He ran faster, desperate to overtake Graves. Desperate to stop him so he couldn't ruin anyone else's life.

Then the shaft opened to the outside.

Jack lowered his torch and stopped for a moment to accustom his eyes to the predawn gloom. He took a step forward, just as a bullet ricocheted off the cave wall beside his head.

He dove back into the cave for protection, but now he had a good idea where Graves was. If only he could keep the man pinned down long enough for Quinn to make his way to help him.

"Give yourself up, Graves. You're surrounded. There's no way to escape."

His offer was answered by another bullet.

"We've got your men, so there's no one coming to help you. It's just you and me and my men. And they're right behind me. You don't have a chance. You're outnumbered and outgunned."

"I'm not going in, Washburn. I know what will happen to me if I'm arrested."

"You knew what your fate would be the moment you smuggled your first load of opium."

"Only if I got caught. And I didn't plan on that happening. I didn't plan on you ever finding my sister."

"She's not your sister. You and she don't share one drop of blood."

"Perhaps not. But it was pleasant thinking of her as my sister," Graves replied. "The only mistake I made was in not killing her before now. I should have known she would never sign over the deed to the land. I should never have let her live this long."

Jack hoped he'd see a sign of Quinn. He didn't know how much longer he could keep Graves occupied.

"Why did you?"

"That hardly matters now. I'll pay for my mistake one way or the other."

"Was it my daughter? Was my daughter the reason you didn't kill her? Was it because my daughter would grow up without a mother, just like you had to grow up without a father?"

"What do you know about how I grew up? Why would I care if your daughter grew up without a mother?"

"Or was it Annie? Do you care for her enough that you couldn't bring yourself to kill her?"

"That hardly matters now."

"No, it doesn't. What matters is that you do one good thing before it's too late. Tell me where my daughter is."

Graves laughed. "Is that what this is about? You want to know where I have your daughter."

"Of course I want to know. I want my daughter back."

"And I want my freedom. That sounds like an even trade to me. Your daughter for my freedom."

"There's not a chance in hell I'll agree to that," Jack answered. "Not after everything you've done."

"That's too bad," Graves said. "She really is a sweet little thing. She's got hair the same color as her mother's."

"Where is she!" Jack demanded.

"My freedom, Washburn! I want my freedom. Once I have that, I'll tell you where your daughter is."

"No! There will be no deal. Not when making a deal with you will guarantee that you'll continue to smuggle opium."

"Then you're going to lose, Washburn, 'cause I'll never tell you where your baby is."

Jack heard a rustling sound from close behind him and turned.

"The only one who is going to lose is you, Colin," Annie said.

Jack stepped out from the cave far enough to see Annie standing close to Graves with a gun in her hand. It was cocked and aimed at the man's back.

"No, Annie. Don't," Jack demanded.

"Why not, Jack? Why shouldn't I kill him?"

"Because you'll have to live with what you did forever. You'll never be able to erase the guilt you'll feel."

"It will be worth it, Jack. After what he's done to me and my baby, it will be worth it."

"No, Annie," Jack said again.

"Listen to your husband, Annie," Graves said. "You don't want to kill me."

She took a step closer to him. "That's where you're wrong,

Colin. I've dreamed of putting a bullet through your heart since you kidnapped me. I've imagined seeing you dead at my feet from the day you took my child away from me. Nothing will give me greater pleasure than to kill you. Nothing!"

"Then you'll never find your baby."

"But I will. I'll search until I do. If it takes my whole life. But you won't be alive to see it. I'll know that all the while I am searching for her, you will be rotting in the ground."

She lifted her arm.

"No, Annie!" Jack shouted.

"All right!" Graves yelled. "She's with my mother. My mother has her."

"No!" Annie screamed. "How could you?"

"What's wrong, Annie?" Jack asked. The look of terror in her eyes told him that something was terribly amiss. "What's wrong?"

"Colin's mother is locked away in a home for the mentally insane."

"What!"

"She's in Radbury House. A home for the insane."

"Bloody hell," Jack said. "I should kill you myself!"

He took a step forward and lifted his gun. Graves answered his threat by lifting his weapon and firing a shot meant to hit Annie. It missed, but before Jack could fire again, Graves dove behind a large boulder.

"Annie, get down!"

Jack waited to catch sight of where Graves was hiding, but he could not be seen.

Suddenly, Graves darted out from behind the boulder to take cover behind another large rock on the hillside.

Jack fired his gun, and so did Quinn, who had just appeared in the mouth of the cave. But their bullets hit the rock and ricocheted away.

Jack fired again, desperate to stop Graves. As long as the man was free, Annie wasn't safe. It was a miracle that he hadn't killed her already.

"Stay down, Annie!" Jack yelled again when he saw Annie attempt to move closer to Graves.

Jack rose to get better aim, and Graves fired. His bullet missed, but Jack took the opportunity to fire.

Graves grabbed his arm as blood soaked through his jacket. He was hit, but not dead. And not severely enough to keep him from escaping.

Jack moved to the other side of the rock he'd been hiding behind and found Quinn, who fired from his position. But Graves was already on the move. Before they could stop him, he made it to his horse.

The thud of hooves sounded in the distance, and Jack knew they'd lost him.

"Damn," Quinn said. "I should have had him. I had a clean shot and missed."

"It's not your fault, Quinn. I had a clean shot too, and I missed him."

"Did he get away?" Annie asked when she came up to them.

Jack gathered her in his arms and held her. "Yes, he got away."

"What are we going to do now?" she asked.

"We're going to get our baby."

"What if Colin gets there first?"

"He's hurt. That will slow him down and give us time to reach our baby before he does. Do you know where this Radbury House is?"

"I do," Jonah answered, coming up to them. "I've been there once or twice."

"All right. Let's go," Jack said, rushing Annie toward the horses. Jonah leaped into the saddle of the farthest horse as Jack mounted and drew Annie up in front of him. In seconds they reached the road and followed Jonah's lead toward Radbury House.

Jack's heart thundered in his chest. They'd come so close to eliminating Graves. If only they had. Now, he would still be a threat to Annie. She would still be in danger.

But he and Annie would have their daughter with them in just a little while. Jack would see and hold his daughter for the first time in his life.

New hope bloomed in his chest. Perhaps they could even be a family.

CHAPTER ELEVEN

JACK HELD ANNIE as best he could as the three raced toward Radbury House. The feel of her against him launched waves of familiarity. He doubted he'd be able to let her go when the time came.

Perhaps he wouldn't have to. When they got their baby back, Annie would need to hold her, and he'd need to hold them both. The anticipation of it was almost more than he could bear.

Jonah led the way. It took them longer than Jack thought it would. It was over an hour from the smugglers' cave.

They finally reached the home for mentally ill patients, and Jack leapt to the ground, then helped Annie down.

"You keep watch, Quinn. Jonah and I will go in."

"Call if you need me," Quinn replied.

Jack took Annie's hand and led her to the house.

"It doesn't look very inviting, does it?" she said, looking to the top of the three-story stone building. The lawn in front of Radbury House was overgrown with weeds and thistles, and the flowerbeds on either side of the walk were filled with dried-up flowers with no blossoms, even though it was the middle of the summer.

"No, it doesn't," Jack answered.

Jonah didn't knock, but opened the door and walked in. Jack and Annie followed him.

The inside looked much the same as the outside, as unkempt and dirty as Jack feared. And his daughter was being raised and cared for here. Anger grew inside him.

"We'll start on the third floor and work our way down," Jonah said.

"Shouldn't we just find someone and ask where our baby is?" Annie suggested.

Jonah shook his head. "No one here will volunteer any information, and before we can stop them, they will have hidden her away so we can't find her."

"Why?"

"Because someone has probably claimed her as their own baby, and they'll fight to keep her."

"Bloody hell," Jack said. "What kind of people run this place?"

"The kind you wouldn't want to take care of your worst enemy. The condition of this place should tell you that."

Annie and Jack followed Jonah to the third floor, and one by one they looked into each room. Before they reached the last room on the third floor, Annie didn't have the stomach to enter another room. She stayed in the hall as Jack and Jonah continued to search.

"I'm sorry," she said when Jack exited the last room on the third floor.

He wrapped his arm around her shoulder and led her to the stairs. "It's all right, sweetheart. You don't have to go into any more rooms."

What he'd seen when he entered the rooms was enough to turn his stomach, too, but what upset him the most was the knowledge that his baby girl had been living in this squalor for at least a year. He couldn't find her soon enough and get her out of this place.

They descended the stairs to the second floor and started their search again.

"There's no sense in both of us searching each room," Jonah said. "Why don't I take the rooms on this side of the hall, and you take the rooms on the other?"

"That's a good idea." Jack turned to Annie. "You stay in the hall and yell if anyone tries to leave, Annie."

She nodded, and they started their search.

They were almost finished with the second floor when Jonah called out for Jack to join him. He raced from the room he was searching and ran to the room across the hall. Annie followed him in.

"What have you found?"

"Look here," Jonah said, pointing to a basket in the corner.

The room was as filthy as every other room they'd gone to, and it had the same smell of urine and unwashed bodies, but there were tiny clothes in the basket. Clothes that belonged to a baby.

"What is it?" Annie asked, looking to where Jonah pointed.

"Someone has been keeping a baby in here," he said.

"Oh, Jack," Annie cried.

"It's all right, sweetheart," Jack replied. "She's here. We've found her."

"Where do you think she is? Someone has her, and they've taken her somewhere."

"Then let's go find her."

"Where?"

"Where would you go on a nice summer day?"

"Outside," Annie cried, then ran to the door.

Jack and Jonah followed her down the stairs, then came to a startling halt when a giant of a woman stepped in front of them. She had to be nearly six feet tall, with shoulders broad enough to intimidate any of the inmates from getting out of hand. If her size didn't stop them, the scowl on her face would.

"What are you doing here?" she bellowed in a deep, gruff voice.

Jonah stepped forward. "Hello. I'm Dr. Reynolds. I've been here before, and I've come back to check on my patient."

"And who would that be?"

"Mrs. Graves. Mr. Colin Graves' mother."

"Why do you need to see her? We didn't send for no doctor."

"I know you didn't, but we just left Colin Graves, and when he discovered we were traveling this way, he asked me to stop in and check on his mother."

"Well, I don't know. We don't usually let strangers in here."

"I can see why," Jonah said in a harsher voice. "From the condition of your patients and their living quarters, the authorities would find enough things wrong here to shut you down and lock you up."

"Bubba!" the lady yelled, and a giant of a man came from another room. "This is Dr. Reynolds, and he's here to see Margaret Graves. She took that brat out to the back garden. Take these people out to see her."

Bubba issued an incoherent grunt, then walked through the dining room. There were dirty dishes still on the tables and a couple of cats cleaning up the scraps of food. From there, he walked out a back door and through an overgrown patch of weeds that served as a garden.

At first Jack didn't see anyone. Then he saw an elderly woman on the ground with a blanket in front of her and a child lying on the blanket.

"Oh," Annie cried out, then started to run toward the woman and the baby.

Jonah held out his hand and stopped her. "Stay here. Let me handle this."

Jack wrapped his arm around Annie's shoulders and held her close to him. He knew why Jonah didn't want Annie to take the baby away from Margaret. If she did, the woman would attack. She'd fight Annie for the baby, and the only one who would get hurt was their daughter.

Jonah turned toward the woman on the blanket. When he drew next to Margaret, he knelt in front of her. "That's a nice baby you have there. What's her name?"

"Baby."

"Oh. Baby. What a beautiful name. Is she a good baby for you?"

"Most of the time, yes. Sometimes, though, she isn't so good. Like when she fusses and I can't get her to stop crying."

"Does she do that often?"

"Na. She's a good baby most of the time."

"What do you do when you can't get her to stop crying?"

"I put her in her box and leave her."

"You leave her?"

"Yes. I close the door and leave her in her box."

"*Ohh…*" Annie cried out.

Jack wrapped his arms around his wife and held her close. She struggled to get free, and he knew she intended to go to her daughter and take her away from the monster who had her. But he couldn't let her. Jonah was right.

Margaret picked Lillie up and clutched her tightly. It was obvious she wasn't going to release her without a fight.

"What if I would get you a baby that didn't cry, Margaret? Would you like that?" Jonah asked.

The woman looked down at the child in her arms.

"What if I could get you a baby who never cried, who never wet her nappy, who you never had to feed, and who would go to sleep as soon as you put her down? Would you like a baby like that?"

"Yes. I'd like that. Can you get me a baby like that?"

"Yes, I can. She'd be the perfect baby."

"I'd like that," Margaret said. She held the child up toward Jonah and just opened her hand. Jonah scooped the baby up as she plummeted to the ground.

He handed the child to Annie, who clutched Lillie in her arms and held her as tears ran down her cheeks.

Jack was overwhelmed by the emotions surging inside him. He held Annie while she held on to their daughter. Tears ran down his face, and he let them flow. What else could he do but let his emotions sweep him away? He was seeing his daughter for the first time in his life.

He stared down at the small bundle in Annie's arms. She looked a great deal like her mother, with blonde hair. But she had his own eyes. They were large and round and midnight blue.

"Now, Margaret," Jonah said to the woman who'd just lost her "baby." "I must go and get your new baby. Will you wait for me to come back with her?"

Margaret frowned. "How long will it take?"

"Until tomorrow?"

"No! I want to keep my baby until you come back with my new baby."

"What if it takes me an hour? I could be back before dinner."

She scrunched her features, and Jack knew her answer was going to be no again.

"And what if I bring you two babies?"

"Two?"

"Yes, two."

"All right," she answered. "Do you promise?"

"I promise."

"You won't forget, will you?"

"No, Margaret. I won't forget. I'll be back as soon as I can, and I'll bring you two babies."

She gave Jonah a big, toothless smile and nodded as if she'd just won a grand prize. And in her world, she had.

Jonah looked over his shoulder and indicated Jack should take Annie and the baby and leave while he kept Margaret occupied, so they did.

When they reached the house, they sped through the filthy interior and rushed to where they'd left Quinn on guard.

"We have our baby, Jack," Annie cried when they were out of the house.

"Yes, we do," Jack replied. He relished the sight of his daughter in Annie's arms, and even though the child needed a bath in the worst way, and most definitely fresh clothes, the two made the most beautiful picture he'd ever seen.

"What did you name her?" Quinn asked.

"LillieBeth. I called her LillieBeth."

"That's perfect. She looks like a Lillie."

The child's resemblance to Annie was remarkable. She had a cute, upturned nose and a round, full face. When she opened her mouth and cried, Jack was sure they could hear her all the way to London. There wasn't a more perfect sound in the whole world.

Quinn helped Jack mount with Annie holding Lillie, then they waited for Jonah to join them. When he arrived, they turned back toward Whitstable. From there, they would go to Burnhaven, but not until they had rested a few days and Jonah had fulfilled his promise to Margaret Graves and given her the two babies he'd promised her.

Jack wrapped his arms around his wife and daughter as they rode. When they reached the road that would take Jonah to the first town large enough to have a shop where he could buy the dolls he'd promised Margaret, he took it.

Jack and Quinn reached Mrs. Walters' by late afternoon and went upstairs. As they expected, Theo was waiting for them.

"What do you have there?" Theo asked.

"I'd like to introduce you to my daughter, Theo," Jack said. "This is Lillie."

"With those eyes, you can't deny she's yours, Jack," Theo said. "She's a beauty."

"Yes, she is," Jack said, looking at his daughter with pride. He was also filled with an emotion he couldn't explain, even though he knew what it was. Love. He loved the little child in Annie's arms. *His* child. A child he didn't know he had until recently.

"Where's Jonah?" Theo asked.

"He's shopping for dolls," Jack answered.

"Dolls?"

"Yes. It's a long story. I'll explain over dinner."

"You can explain while Molly and I give our daughter a much-needed bath," Annie said. "She's desperately in need."

She left the men and took Lillie across the hall to Molly's

room.

"This part of your mission is finally over," Theo said. "What's next?"

Jack walked across the room and filled three glasses with brandy. He gave Theo and Quinn each a glass, then sat in a chair. "I think of it more as now the easy part of our mission is over, and we have to move on to the hard part."

"What do you mean?" Theo asked.

"I need to take Annie to Burnhaven and try to cure her."

"Do you think you'll be able to?"

"I don't know. She's gone through so much already. I'm not sure I can put her through more."

"Didn't you promise you wouldn't force her to give up her laudanum?"

Jack raked his fingers through his hair. "Yes," he said on a sigh. "But I don't know if I can trust her to take care of our baby when she's under its influence."

The looks Theo and Quinn gave him told him they thought the same thing. Annie was a completely different person when laudanum clouded her thinking.

SEVERAL HOURS LATER, Jonah returned from buying and delivering the dolls he'd promised Margaret Graves. Quinn and Theo returned from arranging for charges to be brought against the smugglers Theo and his cohorts had locked up. When they joined Jack, he had already poured them glasses of brandy to celebrate their victory. And it was indeed a victory. Except for the fact that Colin Graves had managed to get away.

"You know Graves is going to exact his pound of flesh," Quinn said as they were eating dinner.

"Yes," Theo agreed. "He's going to make you pay for ruining his smuggling operation."

"You'll have to watch your back until we can find him and stop him," Quinn said, taking a bite of the roast beef on his plate.

"I'll leave the pleasure of finding Graves to you, gentlemen," Jack said, not taking his eyes off the door separating him from his wife and daughter. Graves wasn't the kind of person who would forget what was done to him, and a vengeful fellow was the most dangerous sort of enemy.

While they were still talking, the door opened and Annie entered the room with Lillie in her arms.

"It's time to introduce you to your daughter, Jack. This is what she looks and smells like when she's squeaky clean."

Jack looked at his daughter, and his eyes filled with tears. Her rosebud lips and curly blonde hair had already captivated him, but when the child reached out to grasp his thumb, he was truly captured.

As if she realized she was the center of attention, she babbled incoherently and kicked her little legs with glee.

"Come here, sweet girl," Jack said, slightly lifting the thumb she still held in her little fist. As if she'd known him forever, Lillie nearly leapt out of Annie's arms and into his.

Jack tried unsuccessfully to keep the tears of joy from falling, but couldn't contain them. It was impossible to describe the emotions that consumed him. The love that was undoubtedly transforming him.

He nestled Lillie against him and held the precious bundle that was his daughter.

"To celebrate," Jonah said, handing little Lillie a paper-wrapped package, "I brought you a special gift to remind you of this day."

She grasped the package and crunched the paper in her tiny fists. The crackling sound fascinated her, and she tried to tear at it. She failed with every attempt, and finally Jack ripped the paper for her, and she discovered the soft doll inside.

Lillie hugged the doll and giggled with glee.

"You have a heartbreaker on your hands, Jack," Quinn said

with a broad smile. "You're going to have to lock your daughter up when she gets older. I'm afraid my three boys are going to fight to win her attention."

"One of the first things I'm going to teach Lillie is how to fight off all those boys, then," Jack replied.

"That sounds like an excellent idea," Annie said, and sat down beside him.

"How long are you going to stay in Whitstable?" Theo asked.

Jack looked at Annie and saw the eagerness to go home in her eyes. "I think we'll rest tomorrow, then leave the next morning. Is that all right with you, Annie?"

As if she hadn't thought beyond the moment, Annie's joy seemed to fade the tiniest bit and worry took over.

"Oh. Yes. Yes of course. It will be good to get to Burnhaven."

"Then I think we'll leave with you," Quinn said. "It's time I got home, and I'm sure Theo needs to get home, too."

"Yes, but I have to go to London first and stop in at The Angel's Wings Jams and Jellies," Theo said.

"What is that?" Annie asked.

"Oh," Theo said, "it's a jam and jelly shop my wife and I opened. It helps to support the orphanage we run."

"How remarkable!" She turned to Jack. "We must go there the next time we're in London."

"We most definitely will."

"Oh, look," Quinn said, pointing to Lillie.

She had dropped her little head on Jack's shoulder and fallen asleep, clutching her doll.

"Oh, sweetheart," Annie said, taking her from Jack. "She's had a long day. Hopefully, she'll sleep all night." She walked toward the door that led to the room where she slept. "We're going to go to bed now. We'll see you all in the morning."

"Will you be all right, Annie?"

"Yes, Jack. Molly's waiting for me. She knows what to do."

"Goodnight, sweetheart," Jack said. Theo, Quinn, and Jonah said goodnight, then they all watched her leave the room.

No one spoke for a few moments. Finally, Jonah was brave enough to ask the question Jack knew they were all thinking.

"What are your plans, Jack? Are you going to let your wife continue taking opium?"

Jack raked his fingers through his hair like he was wont to do when he was at a loss for an answer. "I don't know."

"You know it's only going to get worse, don't you?"

He bolted to his feet, annoyed that he'd been put on the spot. "Yes, I know that. But you know what I promised her. You know I told her I wouldn't take her laudanum away from her."

"I know, but by letting her continue as she's doing, she's going to kill herself. She won't be the first person to take too much laudanum and never wake up."

Jack stepped to the window and stared out onto the alley below. "I know," he said, bracing his hands on either side of the window frame.

Jonah stood. "Well," he said, "I have patients to see. I've got to get going. Just know that I'll be here to help you with whatever decision you make."

Jack felt Jonah's supportive fingers clasp his shoulder and knew he'd found a good friend in the doctor.

Jonah opened the door and left. Theo and Quinn were still there, but Jack knew they were about to leave. And he was ready to be alone. He needed to think. He needed to sort out his options and decide what to do.

"Will you be all right, Jack?" Theo asked.

Jack picked up his glass of brandy and took a swallow. "I'll have to be. Won't I?" he answered.

"Remember," Quinn said, placing his hand on Jack's shoulder, "we're here if you need us."

Jack nodded, then watched his friends leave.

He'd never felt more alone in his life.

CHAPTER TWELVE

JACK RENTED A carriage and driver before they left Whitstable so Annie, Lillie, and Molly would be more comfortable as they traveled to Burnhaven. Theo and Quinn rode alongside Jack until they reached the place where Theo turned off to go to London.

Quinn's estate was closer to Burnhaven, so he remained with them.

"How much further is it?" Annie asked after a little while.

"We're almost there," Jack said through the carriage window. "Do you want to stop for a little while?"

"Yes," she answered. "Lillie is starting to fuss. I think she's hungry."

"Very well. There's a good place to rest up ahead. We'll go to those trees and sit in the shade for a little while. Is there any milk left from this morning?" he asked.

They'd stopped at a farmhouse earlier in the day and purchased some milk from the local farmer, and several meat pies the farmer's wife had just baked.

"Yes. Enough for one feeding. And I can mash some of the vegetables in my meat pie. She can eat that."

Jack watched his little family and was filled with an indescribable emotion. Annie was jostling a fussing Lillie on her knees and finding objects for her to play with so she wouldn't cry.

"Here, Annie. Give Lillie to me."

Jack called for the driver to stop the carriage and then reached for Lillie through the window. He nestled her in his lap and urged Comet to move.

Lillie stopped fussing and raised her arms in the air. The soft breeze lifted her hair and ruffled the lapels of her linen coat. She wiggled in Jack's lap and laughed excitedly.

"You're going to enjoy riding, aren't you, Lillie? You're not afraid of horses at all, eh, daughter?"

Lillie not only laughed in answer to his question, but squealed with delight.

He urged Comet to move a little faster, and Lillie's squeals escalated.

Jack kept her on his lap until they reached a grove of trees, then he dismounted and handed Lillie to Annie. They all laughed when Lillie reached out to Comet. It was plain that she wanted to ride again.

"We're going to eat lunch, sweetheart," Annie told her daughter, taking her to the blanket Jack had spread on the ground in the shade beneath an old oak tree.

"I'll take care of the horses," Quinn said, and led the horses to a nearby stream.

Annie handed Lillie to Molly while she got the baby's food ready, then Molly fed Lillie. Lillie drank her milk from their makeshift bottle, then eagerly ate spoonful after spoonful of her vegetables, as if she wasn't used to getting enough to eat. Jack would make sure that never happened again.

Annie watched Lillie eat most of her lunch, then she poured some wine in a glass and added laudanum to it. The amount she added seemed like more than he'd seen Jonah give her, but Jack couldn't say with any certainty. Perhaps it wasn't.

"How long until we reach Burnhaven?" Annie asked as they ate their meat pies.

"We should be there in a few hours," Jack answered. He leaned back on the blanket and let the sunshine warm him.

Quinn came back from watering the horses and sat down

beside them to eat his own dinner.

"I imagine you're anxious to get home, too," she said to Quinn.

"Yes. I don't like to be gone from my family for too long." He smiled. "I never thought I'd say this, but I miss them."

Jack saw the seriousness on Quinn's face and knew what he meant. He'd only been with his wife and daughter for a short period of time, but couldn't imagine leaving them for very long at all.

He watched Molly feed Lillie the last of the mashed vegetables from her meat pie, then his daughter drank the rest of her milk. It wasn't long after she'd eaten that Lillie fell asleep in Molly's arms.

Jack watched his daughter sleep, then shared a look with Annie. It was obvious that the laudanum was taking effect already. There was a glassy look in her eyes that indicated she was under the influence of her medicine, and she appeared much more relaxed than she had a few minutes earlier. Jack was now quite adept at recognizing the signs when Annie had taken laudanum.

"It's a miracle she survived living with Margaret Graves," Annie said.

"She's quite healthy for what she's gone through," Quinn commented. "Exactly how old is she, Annie?"

"She was born on the fourteenth of June, exactly one year ago last month," Annie answered.

"She should be walking soon. Just wait until she starts running. You'll have your hands full trying to keep up with her."

"Are your boys walking?" she asked.

Quinn laughed. "I don't think they ever walked. My wife swears they skipped that part and went straight to running."

Annie laughed lazily at Quinn's joke. "I don't envy you, or your wife," she said. "You must have a very lively house."

"We do. Jack will have to bring you over when you get settled at Burnhaven."

"Yes," she yawned. "Yes, he will."

Quinn leaned back on the blanket and looked as if he had a dozen questions he wanted to ask.

"What is it?" she asked him.

"Would you mind telling me how long you were held captive, and how long you were given the 'medicine' you took every day?"

Jack slid close enough that he could wrap his arm around Annie and give his sleepy wife support. He knew speaking about what she'd gone through wasn't easy for her, but he didn't mind Quinn asking. Maybe he would understand better why it was so difficult for her to give up the drug.

"Jack was sent on an assignment the first week of October, and I was left alone at Burnhaven. Everything was fine until Colin Graves showed up. He brought a fake deed for the land he wanted me to sign over to him. When I refused, the men with him took me away from Burnhaven and locked me in a house with his mother."

"You had to live with Margaret Graves?" Jack asked her.

Annie nodded. "That's when I realized how ill she was and how demented she was. A few weeks after that, I realized I was pregnant."

She reached for her glass of wine and added two more drops of laudanum to it, then took a drink.

"I hid my pregnancy as long as I could. I was afraid Colin would use the baby to force me to sign over the deed to the land, so I tried to keep it from him that I was with child. But I couldn't conceal it forever. Eventually, he realized I was going to have a baby, and he became furious. He threatened to kill Lillie when she was born, but thankfully, his mother fought him. She called Lillie her dolly and protected her just like you saw when we were at Radbury. She wouldn't let Colin near me."

"That's a good thing," Jack said. "Otherwise, I'm afraid Colin would have hurt Lillie."

He looked at his wife again. It was obvious she had something else to reveal.

"What is it, Annie?" he asked.

"Lillie's birth was difficult. I almost didn't survive it. I lost a large amount of blood and was ill for several weeks. That's when Mrs. Graves started giving me laudanum again. She called it my elixir. It helped with the pain, and I was glad to take it."

"How long have you taken it?"

"From when Lillie was born until now."

"So, a little more than a year," Quinn said.

"Yes."

"No wonder you crave it. Your body is telling your mind that you need it."

"I do need it. It helps me forget what I went through."

Quinn shared a look with Jack that told him it wasn't going to be easy to convince Annie to give up something she relied so fiercely upon. But Jack already knew that. He only hoped that someday Annie would realize that she was missing out on so much of life with him and her daughter when she was under the opium's control.

They sat there a while longer and talked, mostly about Quinn's family and what raising five children was like. Annie listened intently, though her eyelids continued to droop. She'd always said she wanted a large family, but Jack wasn't sure that was possible any longer. How could she raise several children when she could hardly take care of herself in this condition?

"We need to get going," he said. "We're close enough to Burnhaven that we should be there in a few hours."

"And I'm close enough to Rosemont to be home about the same time as you reach Burnhaven," Quinn added.

Annie reached for Jack's hand. "I can't wait, Jack. It seems like it's been a lifetime since we've been home."

"I feel the same," he said, then pulled Annie to her feet. When she was upright, he helped her into the carriage, then gave Lillie to Molly. From the look of her, Annie would be asleep the moment the carriage began to rock. They told Quinn goodbye, then continued on to Burnhaven, making good time.

It was just under three hours before they reached Burnhaven's tree-lined lane. The turn roused Annie, and she seemed excited as they went under the wrought-iron arch with the large **B** on it, then rode to the front of the mansion.

There was something very emotional about coming home after a long journey. Jack had missed his home more than he thought he would. And this time, he vowed he would not leave it so easily again.

He'd left Annie once before, and tragedy had struck. He wasn't about to take a chance with her or with Lillie. They were much too important to him. He was responsible for them. He'd taken a vow to love and protect them, and he wasn't about to ignore that vow. Especially now that he had Lillie.

ANNIE WALKED THROUGH her home. It had been nearly two years since she'd lived here. Two years since she'd walked these halls and slept in their bed. Two years since she and Jack had made love under this roof, and she'd missed that more than anything.

The first thing they did was to show Molly to her room. The look on her face was priceless. This was the first time the girl had ever had a room of her own. Someday, when Molly had been with them for a while and she felt comfortable around them, Annie intended to ask her what her life had been like before she came to help her.

From the little Molly had shared, Annie knew her life hadn't been easy.

"Oh," Molly sighed when she walked into the room that would be hers.

"Do you like it, Molly?"

"Oh, mistress. It's the most beautiful room I've ever seen. It's as grand as a room for a princess."

Annie looked at Jack, and they shared a smile. "I'm glad you like it. It's been a long day so far. You can freshen up and take a nice, long nap in your new bed. You can join us when you wake."

"Oh my." Molly sighed. "I can't believe I'm so lucky."

"Well, you are. You rest for a while, and we'll call you for dinner."

"Thank you, mistress. Thank you, Major."

"You're welcome, Molly," Jack said, then they left her to enjoy her new room.

Annie clutched her husband's arm as he took her on a tour through the house. He led her through the halls, into each of the sitting rooms, then the dining room and the library, then out onto the terrace.

"Are you glad to be home?" he asked as they walked a narrow garden path.

"I'd forgotten what it felt like to be this happy," she answered.

"I'll never forget the look on your face earlier when we walked through the front entrance," he said, wrapping his arm around her shoulders and pulling her close to him.

"You mean you'll never forget that I cried like a baby when I walked through the door," Annie huffed.

"It was a charming sight."

Jack stopped and turned her in his arms, then leaned down and kissed her.

His kisses had always affected her with an emotion so powerful they melted her from the inside out, and this one was no different. Annie's legs threatened to give out beneath her, and her heart pounded in her breast.

She wrapped her arms around his neck and pulled him close to her. She couldn't allow even one whisper of breath to separate them. That would be too much. She needed him so close to her that they seemed to be one person.

Jack deepened his kiss as a plea for Annie to be the other half of him.

She let her kisses speak for her. She let her kisses express her love for him. How was it possible for her to love someone this much? How could she have found the perfect match to what she'd been missing?

Annie lifted her lips from Jack's and pressed her cheek to his chest below his chin. His heart thundered so hard that she heard and felt it as if it were beating in her own breast.

"Come," he said through his ragged breathing. "I want to see Lillie. I want to see her in her own bed, in her own room. In her home where she belongs."

Annie walked beside Jack as they entered Lillie's room. She was sleeping in her bed, and the groundsman's wife Jack had pressed into emergency service to watch over the baby was sitting beside her.

"Good afternoon, Mrs. Crawford," Annie said.

"Good afternoon, Mrs. Washburn. Major Washburn."

"Did you have any trouble putting Lillie down for a nap?"

"None at all. She fell asleep as soon as her little head hit the pillow. I think she knew she was home where she belonged."

Jack wrapped his arm around his wife's shoulders. "We're all home where we belong, aren't we, Annie?" he said.

"Yes," she said, looking up at her husband. "Yes we are. Do you need anything, Mrs. Crawford?"

"No. I have everything I need."

"Good," Annie said. "I'll have Cook send up a tray for you in a little while."

"Thank you, ma'am."

Jack and Annie watched their baby sleep a moment longer, then left to tour the rest of the house.

"Tell me again how you acquired this house, and the estate."

"Will you never get tired of hearing the story?"

"Never," she answered. "It tells me just how brave you were, and how much the queen appreciated what you did for your country."

"Well," Jack said, leading her down the staircase to the

ground floor, "Quinn and I had been ordered to infiltrate the enemy's camp and steal the battle plans the Russians intended to use to defend the port city of Sevastopol. The battle had already raged for over ten months, and the losses on both sides were monumental. Quinn stood guard outside the tent while I went in to find the battle plans. I retrieved them, and he and I took them back to our commander. It gave us a huge advantage over the next few weeks, and we finally emerged victorious."

Annie wrapped her arm around Jack's waist and walked with him to the library. When they reached the library, they exited through the double French doors onto the terrace. Once there, they walked across the terrace, down the steps, and took the center path to the small pond where they found a shaded bench.

"All I have to say," Annie said, resting her head on Jack's shoulder, "is that it's a good thing I read the true account of your heroism in the papers and know what you did. What you endured. You make it sound like it was a Sunday walk through Hyde Park, when I know you were captured and beaten, and your bravery saved thousands of lives."

"Newspapers have a tendency to sensationalize events."

"I don't think they did so in this case. You forget, I've seen the scars from your 'walk through Hyde Park.'"

Jack leaned over and kissed her on the cheek.

"Very well," Annie said. "Continue. Finish your story. That's the best part."

"Well," Jack said on a laugh, "when I returned to Britain, the queen commanded an audience and asked me what reward I wanted for my contribution to bringing the war to an end, and I asked for a small plot of land with a cottage on it. And the queen deeded me Burnhaven Estate."

"Yes," Annie said on a sigh. "Now we have the most amazing small cottage any family could wish for."

"Yes," he said, and kissed her again.

They sat on the bench and watched the geese and ducks swim in the pond in front of them.

"Do you think Colin will leave us alone, Jack? Or will he come after us for what we did to him?"

"I don't know, Annie. I'd like to think he's smart enough to get as far away from here as possible and leave us alone, but something tells me he's not that smart."

"That's what I fear, too. We've ruined him and any hope he had to get rich."

"He's a very vindictive person, and not one to forgive and forget," Jack said.

"What are we going to do about him?"

"I've hired several guards to keep him out of Burnhaven. You'll be safe, Annie."

"I'm not worried about me, Jack. I'm worried about you. You're the one he'll try to destroy."

He smiled. "Don't worry about me. I'll be fine."

But Annie knew Jack was in the most danger.

They sat a little while longer, then Annie pulled away from her husband. "We need to go in. Cook no doubt has dinner ready, and I'm starving."

"No doubt," Jack said, then stood and extended Annie his hands and pulled her to her feet. "Do you know what we're having tonight for dinner?"

"Beef roast with potatoes and carrots. And for dessert, warm apple pie. All your favorites."

"The food is the best part of being home. After eating army rations for nearly three years, I enjoy everything Cook fixes."

When they reached the house, Jack led her into the small dining room. The meal was indeed delicious, and they ate it with gusto before retiring to the library.

Jack poured himself a glass of brandy, and Annie a glass of wine. Annie reached in her pocket, took out a small vial, and poured a liberal amount of laudanum into her wine.

He watched what she did, but didn't criticize. It seemed an act of kindness, and she loved him for it. Annie wondered how long it would take before she felt comfortable taking her medicine in front of him.

She was consumed by guilt. Guilt because she knew being dependent on it made her weak. Guilt because she knew Jack didn't like what she was doing, yet didn't reprimand her for her weakness. And guilt because the amount that used to calm her nerves and allow her to escape into that ethereal world where nothing was real and nothing bothered her was no longer enough. Now, it took more than it ever had. What used to allow her to forget the horrors of her imprisonment no longer shut out her nightmares. Nor did her euphoric calmness last nearly as long as it used to.

Annie took a large swallow of the mixture, then rose from her chair and walked to the shelves of books, feigning interest in choosing one that would hold her interest. Nothing did, but how could she enjoy her glass of wine when she knew Jack was watching her, was judging her?

Annie took another swallow. She needed it to stop the guilt she experienced knowing that, even though he didn't say anything, Jack was judging her for her dependence on her medicine.

She drained the wine in her glass. She'd think about it all later. Right now she'd just stay adrift.

❧

CHAPTER THIRTEEN

THE DAYS AT Burnhaven went by in idyllic tranquility. There was only one wrinkle in what would otherwise have been a perfect respite—and that was the way Annie felt when she started each day.

She woke every morning and struggled to clear her head. She had Molly trained to have a cup of coffee waiting when she rose. She needed it to help her function at first.

Things turned better after she had her first dose of medicine. Only then was she assured she could face the day.

Once she rose, she dressed, then went to the nursery to spend time with Lillie. Her little darling was growing like the proverbial weed, and, like Annie had suspected, she skipped the walking stage and went right to running. It took both Molly and Mrs. Crawford to keep up with her. It took both of them to keep her entertained.

Usually when Annie got to Lillie's room, she was eating breakfast and Annie was able to feed her, then play with her for a while until she became tired and was ready for her morning nap. Today, Annie was a little late, and Lillie was just finishing her breakfast.

She took Lillie from Mrs. Crawford and sat with her on her lap. She played pat-a-cake with her, then sang a little ditty before handing her back to Mrs. Crawford. Lillie loved it when Annie sang to her, and every once in a while she would even sing along with her mother.

Of course, she wasn't really singing—she was too young to say any words or carry a tune—but she did coo. And Annie loved it.

As she did each morning, she left Lillie in Mrs. Crawford's care and went to the small breakfast room to eat with Jack.

"Lillie sang with me again this morning," she announced when she entered the room, and Jack laughed.

"She *did*," Annie insisted as she filled her plate with eggs, bacon, and a piece of toasted bread. She knew she would never eat all the food she took, but he questioned her when he didn't think she was eating enough. "I know she didn't really sing, but she made noises like she was trying to sing."

He smiled as he finished his coffee, then slid his cup and saucer back. "So, what are your plans for today?"

"I'm going to spend the day with Lillie. It's going to be our special day. Just the two of us. It's a perfect day for a walk in the garden, then a picnic."

"She'll love it."

"Would you like to join us? I have a new book to read to our daughter. It's about a very talented rabbit."

"I would love to hear about this talented rabbit, but I'm afraid I've avoided meeting with my land steward and working on the ledgers long enough. I can't put off work any longer."

"If you must," Annie teased as she sat, "but you're going to regret missing out on our story. It's quite enthralling."

"I'm sure it is, but if I get started on the books right now, I may need to take a break in time to join you for your picnic."

"Lillie would love that," Annie said, then leaned over and gave Jack a kiss on the cheek. "And so would I."

"Then I'll make sure I add your picnic into my day."

She placed her napkin on the table beside her plate and rose.

"Where are you going, Annie? You haven't eaten yet."

Annie looked at the food still on her plate and realized she hadn't even taken a bite. "I... Um... I..."

"Sit down, Annie."

She sat again, then lifted her gaze to meet Jack's.

"How much did you take this morning, Annie?"

"I'm fine, Jack. I just forgot what I wanted to do for a moment."

Annie tried to keep her voice level, but even to her own ears, her voice was strident. She sounded angry. And she knew Jack recognized her words for the lie they were. She hadn't only forgotten what she *wanted* to do, she'd forgotten what she *was* doing.

"Please, Annie. Be—"

"Don't criticize me, Jack! I know what I'm doing. You don't need to watch me like I need a caretaker."

"I'm just worried about you, Annie. I'm afraid you—"

"Leave me alone, Jack!" She slid her chair back so forcefully it tipped over. "Just leave me alone!" she cried, and stormed out of the room.

JACK STARED IN shock as Annie left the room. Things were getting worse. When he'd received the letter telling him that she was alive, the only important thing was that he might get back the other half of his heart. He'd convinced himself that he could endure any changes in Annie as long as she was back with him. He'd convinced himself that once they were together, their love would be enough for her. That she wouldn't need her "medicine" anymore.

But those dreams were far from how life really was.

The woman who called herself his wife wasn't at all like the woman he'd married. Annie was a stranger to him, someone he barely knew. This woman wasn't in control of her actions. She was taking much more laudanum than when he first found her.

Jack raked his fingers through his hair, then rose from his chair. He needed to think. He needed to consider his best course of action. He needed to decide what was best for his wife.

But he had no idea what that was.

Jack went to his study and sat behind his desk. He'd intended to get so much done today, but he was no longer in the mood to meet with his land steward, or work on his ledgers. Instead, he stood and stared out the window.

He didn't know how long he stood looking out at nothing in particular, but knew it was more than just a few minutes. Perhaps even an hour.

"Jack?"

He turned.

Annie stood inside the room. She wore a yellow gown as bright as the sun. Her cheeks were rosy, and her hair was loosely pulled back, leaving several wispy tendrils to frame her heart-shaped face. Her eyes were wide and looked at him as if she could see deep into his soul. She was the most beautiful creature God had ever created. And heaven help him, but he loved her.

"I'm sorry, Jack."

He took a step toward her and reached out his hands. He wanted her in his arms. He was desperate to hold her, desperate to keep her safe from the poison that was eating away at her. Desperate for his love to be enough to change her back into the woman he'd married.

She lifted her skirt and ran to him.

Jack gathered her to him and held her close, then covered her mouth with his and kissed her with all the love her felt for her.

"I'm sorry, Jack," she said when he broke their kiss. "I'm so sorry. I'll be better. I won't take so much. I'll cut way back. You'll see. I don't know what came over me. I lost control. I won't do that ever again."

"Oh, Annie. That's all I want."

"I know. I know. I'll be better. You'll see."

"I love you, Annie. I just want us to be like we were before."

"So do I, Jack. So do I. I love you. I could never survive without you. I love you too much."

He kissed her again. This time she returned his kiss with a passion that was real. Not a drug-induced passion that contained little emotion.

"Why don't you get Lillie and take her out to the garden? That's what you said you wanted to do. I'll work on my ledgers for a while, then join you when it's time for lunch."

"That sounds perfect," she said, then gave him a final kiss on the cheek and left to get Lillie.

⟫⟫⟫⟪⟪⟪

OVER THE NEXT several weeks, good days mixed with bad, and though he tried not to worry about her, Jack found himself reluctant to leave Annie alone. He met with his land steward daily, but always in his study. And he never rode the land with the man. He didn't trust Annie enough to be gone that long. He especially didn't trust her to be alone with Lillie.

There were days when he thought she was in control of the amount of laudanum she took, then there were days when he knew she wasn't. Those were the days that frightened him most.

He wasn't sure what kind of day today was. He hadn't seen her yet this morning. She must have slept late, or was still playing with Lillie.

Just when he was about to go to the nursery to see if Annie was there, the door to his study opened and she walked in with Lillie in her arms.

"Your daughter insisted on coming down to tell her father good morning, didn't you, Lillie?"

"And a very good morning to you, Lillie. What are you and Mummy planning to do today?"

He stood and took Lillie from Annie. He was glad. This seemed as though it was going to be a good day for Annie. Her gaze wasn't glassy like it was some mornings, and her speech wasn't as slow and slurred as it was when she was under the influence.

"We thought we'd sit in the garden for a while. The weather is too gorgeous to let such a perfect day go to waste. Can you join us?"

"My steward is going to stop by in a little while. We have some details to discuss, but they shouldn't take too long. I'll join you as soon as we're finished."

"Wonderful," Annie answered.

Jack gave his daughter a kiss on the cheek, then handed her back to his wife. "I can't get over how she's growing," he said when Annie took her back.

"I know. Sometimes I think I've missed out on such a large part of her life."

"You did, Annie. And so did I."

"Yes, you did. All thanks to Colin. Have your men seen any sign of him?"

Jack shook his head, then walked them to the double doors that led to the terrace, then to the garden. "You ladies have a great morning," he said as Annie put Lillie on the ground and they walked hand in hand until they were out of sight.

He returned to his study to find his steward waiting. They discussed adding more sheep to their growing number and selling the wool the sheep produced. Then Jack asked his steward's advice on what crops to plant next spring. The man had read a great article on the advantages of rotating crops every year and thought that made a great deal of sense. They'd rotated several fields last year, and the steward was quite excited about how the yields looked in the fields where they'd tried it.

When they finished, the steward left, and Jack rose to join Annie and Lillie. He turned toward the terrace door just as Annie entered his study. She was alone.

Her eyes were glassy, and Jack knew immediately that she'd taken much more than she'd promised.

"Annie, where's Lillie?"

"What? You don't have to shout. I can hear you."

"Where's Lillie? Where is she?"

Jack looked at the blank expression on his wife's face. She had no idea where their little girl was. She had no idea what he was even talking about.

Jack bolted out the French doors and ran down the pebbled path.

"Lillie!" he yelled. "Lillie!"

He ran until he came to Lillie's blanket on the ground. But she wasn't on it, nor was she anywhere around it. He turned and focused on the pond where the ducks and geese swam. She loved to play in the water.

Panic began to set in as he ran the short distance to the pond and scanned its shallow depths. There she was! Halfway across the pond, her arms paddling, her legs kicking. She was struggling to keep her head above water, but she couldn't. As he plunged into the pond, her little blonde head lifted from the water one more time, then she stopped struggling and lay face down and didn't move.

"Lillie!" Jack yelled as he plowed through the water and reached out for her. He snatched her up and carried her to dry ground, then placed her over his shoulder and pounded her back until she released the water trapped in her lungs.

She took in one breath, then another, then opened her mouth and let out a pitiful wail. It was the most wonderful sound he'd ever heard.

"Is she all right?" Annie asked as she arrived. She stood next to him and wrung her hands in front of her.

"Get away from her, Annie. You get away from her!"

Her hands flew to cover her mouth, her eyes filled with tears, and she took a few steps back from him.

"Can I hold her, Jack? I need to hold her."

"No, you may not hold her! I've got her!"

He rocked his precious baby in his arms and ran to the blanket that still lay on the ground. With the tenderest care he shushed Lillie's fearful cries and wrapped the blanket around her.

"Please," Annie said.

"No!"

Jack watched as Mrs. Crawford and Molly ran toward them.

"Is the baby all right?" Mrs. Crawford asked, wiping tears from her eyes.

"Yes, she will be," he answered. "Come with me. Both of you."

"Yes, Major."

"Molly, warm some milk for Lillie. And if Cook has a biscuit left, bring that with you."

"Yes, Major."

Jack nestled a crying Lillie as close as he could and carried her to her room. Mrs. Crawford followed on his heels, and when they reached the nursery, she took out some dry clothes and helped him change the baby.

He looked up to see Annie standing in the open doorway. He stormed across the room and slammed the door in her face.

He'd never been so angry in his life. He'd never been so frightened in his life. Lillie had almost died. She *could* have died. All because Annie was so dependent on laudanum that she'd left their daughter alone and forgotten all about her.

Jack leveled upon Mrs. Crawford the most lethal expression he could summon. "Mrs. Crawford. My wife is *never* to go anywhere near my daughter. You are *never* to let Lillie out of your sight."

"Yes, Major. But—"

"No! My wife is never to be with our daughter unless you are there to supervise them. Is that understood?"

"Yes, Major."

Molly came with the warm milk and several biscuits, and Jack fed Lillie himself, teasing her with them to distract her from the recent trauma. When her biscuit was gone, he rocked her. It didn't take long and she was fast asleep. He held her a little while longer, reluctant to lay her down.

He'd nearly lost his daughter. If he had been a few minutes later, he would have. All because Annie couldn't be trusted to keep her wits about her. All because the feeling she got from her *medicine* was more important to her than her child.

He placed Lillie in her bed, then left the room. He regretted what he had to do now. He had to confront Annie. He had to tell his wife he would no longer allow her to be alone with Lillie. He had to tell the mother of his child that she couldn't be alone with her daughter. But he had no choice.

Lillie had been lucky this time. She'd survived. But that didn't mean she would the next time Annie was so negligent. The next time he might be burying his daughter instead of feeding her biscuits and milk.

Chapter Fourteen

ANNIE SAT IN Jack's study and waited for him to join her. She knew he would. She dreaded that he would, because she knew how angry he was with her. And he deserved to be angry with her. Their baby daughter could have died.

Why had she taken so much laudanum? Sometimes she just couldn't control the amount she thought she needed. And, even more frightening, there were times when she couldn't remember when she'd already taken it. So she'd take it again.

She knew Jack had tried to confiscate her supply of laudanum, but she had vials hidden in places where he'd never find them. She didn't trust him. Even though he'd assured her that he would never take it completely away from her, she didn't trust him enough to believe that the day wouldn't come when she woke up to find he'd destroyed her entire cache.

It wasn't difficult to amass a large quantity of the precious stuff. She couldn't ask Molly to go to town to purchase it because she didn't trust the girl enough to believe that she wouldn't inform Jack what Annie had ordered her to do.

But Molly was only one of the Burnhaven staff who could get her what she needed. There were the stable hands, the gardeners, and footmen who couldn't disobey her orders to go to the village to make her special purchase.

Annie thought how easy it was to get more. Easier than even

Jack realized it was.

Angry footsteps stomped across the tiled marble foyer, nearing his study. She clutched her hands tightly in her lap and squeezed her eyes shut. She waited until the door opened, then listened as it closed with a firm thud.

Annie didn't lift her gaze. She couldn't force herself to look at him.

Jack went to the bottles of liquor and filled a glass. He took several swallows, then set the glass back down on the table.

"What do you intend to do, Annie?"

She refused to be cowed by him, refused to show weakness. She knew if she did, he'd destroy her.

"I don't know what you mean, Jack. I know what happened was unfortunate, but—"

Jack picked up his glass and threw it against the stones in the fireplace. The glass shattered with a deafening explosion. "*Unfortunate!* You think what happened was *unfortunate?* You nearly killed our daughter! That's much more than unfortunate, Annie!"

She felt as if Jack had slapped her. Her resolve to remain strong fell apart. The tears she swore she would not allow to fall spilled from her eyes and ran down her cheeks like swollen rivers.

He was correct. It was her fault Lillie had nearly died. It was her fault Lillie had fallen in the pond and nearly drowned. Everything was her fault.

Annie wrapped her arms around her waist and rocked back and forth. She needed Jack to understand. She needed him to sit down beside her and hold her and tell her everything would be all right.

But he didn't.

He remained where he was and kept the icy look of fury on his face and in his eyes. For the first time, she realized Jack would never forgive her for what she'd allowed to happen. She'd done the unforgivable. She'd crossed a line, and it was impossible to step back.

He glared at her for several long, unforgiving minutes and said nothing before turning his back on her.

Annie's heart shattered in her breast, and she felt more alone than she'd ever been. For the first time in her life, she was afraid she'd lost him. She was terrified that she had destroyed any chance they had to rekindle the love they'd once had for each other. And she didn't know how she would survive if he abandoned her. She knew she couldn't live without him.

"What happens now?" she asked him, knowing that he alone determined their future.

"From this day forward, you will never be allowed to spend any time alone with our daughter, Annie. Mrs. Crawford, Molly, or I will be with you whenever you even look at our daughter. You will be supervised every second you are with Lillie."

"You can't—"

He turned back around and glared at her. The look in his eyes was the blackest look of disapproval she'd ever seen. The man facing her wasn't the man she'd fallen in love with, the kind, gentle man she'd married. There wasn't a hint of kindness or forgiveness in his look.

"I can! I am the only parent I trust to care for our daughter. Definitely not you! You and your sickness have proven you cannot be trusted."

"How long do you intend to keep me away from Lillie?"

"Forever, Annie! Forever, or until you no longer take a drop of that blasted stuff!"

"You can't mean that!"

"Oh, I mean it. You decide what you want more—to be a mother to our daughter, or to continue to poison your body and your mind."

"You're a heartless bastard!"

"If I am, it's you who made me this way. You nearly killed my daughter! I can never forgive you for that!" he yelled, and walked out on her.

>>><<<

ANNIE TRIED TO visit Lillie every day but was met with resistance, whether from Mrs. Crawford or from Jack. It seemed that he spent more time with Lillie than away from her. Every time Annie entered her baby's room, Jack had Lillie in his arms and was rocking her, or playing with her. He allowed Annie to sit beside him and look at Lillie, but she was not allowed to touch her or hold her or rock her.

"How long is this going to last, Jack?"

"Until Lillie is old enough to protect herself from you and not have to depend on you to keep her safe."

"You can't mean that, Jack."

"Oh, I mean it. I definitely mean every word of it."

She focused on her husband. He was still the most handsome man she'd ever met, but he'd changed. He used to smile and laugh and tease her with the most outrageous pranks. Now she couldn't remember the last time he'd smiled at her, or teased her, or shown any interest in her. She could point to the exact moment his good humor had disappeared and was replaced by anger and a desire to make her suffer for her mistake. Or her weakness.

"What do I have to do, Jack?"

He lifted his gaze and focused on her with a look that burned through her. "You know what you have to do, Annie."

"Are you saying you won't let me near my daughter until I stop taking my medicine?"

"Stop calling it that, Annie! It's not *medicine*. It's a drug. It's opium!"

Annie swallowed back the tears that threatened to fall. "I can't, Jack. I'm not strong enough."

"You *are* strong enough, Annie. If you could just make that decision, I'd be with you every step of the way. We'd conquer it. Together. But—"

Jack shrugged and rose and put a sleeping Lillie in her bed, then went to Annie and knelt in front of her. He reached for her hands and held them in his. His hold communicated all the strength she knew he would give her.

"We can do this, Annie. I'll make sure we do. We can't fail. Lillie needs her mother. And I need my wife."

With tears running down her cheeks, she shook her head. "I can't," she said, rising from the bed. She stepped past him, then gave him her back and left the room.

JACK STARED AT the closed door for several moments after Annie walked away from him. A heavy weight refused to lift from his chest. How could he survive a lifetime without her at his side? He wasn't sure he could. How could his daughter survive without her mother?

He swiped his hand down his face and sank into the nearest chair. He knew what he needed to do. His only choice was to continue as he had been. For Lillie's safety, he couldn't allow Annie to take the baby where she wasn't watched. Their daughter would never be safe with her mother. Not as long as she continued to take laudanum.

Jack pushed himself to his feet and walked to the door. He motioned for Mrs. Crawford to return to watch Lillie, then he walked down the stairs and went to his study.

He poured himself a glass of brandy, then paced the floor. He knew Annie thought he was being unreasonable. She didn't understand how he could keep her away from her daughter, how he could be so cruel. Yet what choice did he have?

The next time she left Lillie unattended, he might not be as fortunate as he'd been that day at the pond. Lillie could have drowned. She could have been dead before he reached her.

No, let Annie hate him. Let her think he was cruel. At least

Lillie would be alive.

Even if his marriage was dead.

ANNIE LOOKED OUT of the window to where Molly and Mrs. Crawford were playing with Lillie in the garden. Molly ran after Lillie, and when she caught her, she lifted the child in the air and swung her around.

Lillie's laughter was almost loud enough to be heard all the way to the house. She giggled and giggled, and when Molly put her down, she turned in dizzy circles and plopped on her bottom.

The pain Annie felt watching her baby laugh and play while knowing she could never be a part of her life hurt her more than she could put into words.

It had been nearly six weeks since Jack issued his edict that Annie wasn't allowed to be anywhere near Lillie unless someone was there to supervise her. She could watch, as she was doing now, but she could not go near her daughter unless he was there to watch over her.

She almost hated him—almost. How could he be so heartless? How could he be so cruel? Did he hate her that much?

But she knew he didn't. He was only keeping her away from their daughter because he loved Lillie that much. And she knew he was correct.

When she was in a drugged state, she hated him for what he was doing to her. But when her medicine wore off, she realized he was right. He'd made the right decision. She wasn't responsible enough to keep Lillie safe.

Annie focused on their child again. Mrs. Crawford stood near the pond and held Lillie in her arms. Molly had a hunk of bread and tore off pieces that she threw to the swans. The swans dove for the pieces of bread, and when their heads came out of the water, Lillie laughed and shrieked with excitement.

Just then, Jack walked down another path and met them. The second Lillie saw him, she wiggled in Mrs. Crawford's arms and reached out for her father. He swept her up in his arms and swung her around, then lifted her above his head while she squealed with joy.

Annie's eyes filled with tears as she watched him interact with their daughter. A sharp pain stabbed at her heart. Lillie would have such fond memories of Jack playing with her, spending time with her, and all the other things he did with her that Annie wasn't allowed to do except when he was present.

Annie was missing out on so much. Lillie would never know her in the same way she would know and remember Jack. That thought made her ill. That thought hurt her more than anything else.

Her heart grew heavy and pressed in her breast.

Only she could change how her daughter remembered her. Only she had the power to make her own life different than it was now. All she had to do was…

Tears spilled from her eyes and streamed down her cheeks. They refused to stop. They refused to even slow. Then, somewhere in the back of her mind, a commanding voice issued the questions she'd never allowed herself to hear. Never allowed herself to answer.

How badly do you want to be a part of your daughter's life? What do you love more? Your daughter or your medicine?

Annie swiped the tears from her cheeks and looked at the French doors when they opened and Jack entered the room.

"Annie?" he asked. "Are you all right?"

She shook her head. "I can't go on like this, Jack."

He closed his eyes and breathed a heavy sigh. "Only you can make things different."

"I know." More tears spilled. "Will you help me, Jack?"

"You know I will." He wrapped his arms around her and held her.

"Don't let me go, Jack."

"I won't, Annie. I'll never let you go. I love you too much."

"And I love you," she replied, and lifted her chin to meet Jack's mouth when he lowered his head to kiss her. "What will we do now?" she asked when Jack lifted his lips from hers.

"We write Jonah. We ask him to come and be with us. No one knows more about this than he does. And he'll help us."

"Will you write to him?"

"Yes. I'll ask him to come."

Annie locked gazes with her husband. "Hold me, Jack. I need you to hold me."

Jack gathered Annie in his arms and held her. He was all strength and muscle. All warmth and power. Total might and potency. He was everything she wanted and needed. Exactly what she'd fallen in love with. The only man she would ever love.

She wrapped her arms around his waist and held him tight.

She could do this. With Jack at her side, she could do this.

At least, she prayed she could.

IT HAD BEEN four days since Jack had sent Jonah a letter. Annie expected the doctor to arrive anytime.

She spent as much time as she could with Lillie every day. She held her, fed her, and took long walks with her. Of course, Jack or Molly or Mrs. Crawford always accompanied her. Her husband still didn't trust her to watch over their tiny daughter without something happening to her.

She and Jack and Lillie went on a picnic every day, and they sat out beneath a large shade tree and talked and played with Lillie. As soon as their baby fell asleep, she and Jack would kiss, then make love.

Every evening before she retired for the night, she and her husband would take a leisurely stroll through the garden. They would stop and watch the moon and the stars for a time. Then they'd enjoy a glass of wine before they went to bed.

They made love incessantly because Annie wanted to store up memories of Jack holding her, Jack touching her, and Jack inside her.

But, no matter how desperate she was to stop time from moving forward, the days and nights continued to speed by until early one morning, Jonah arrived.

"Jonah," Jack greeted their friend. "Come in. Have a seat."

The doctor entered the drawing room where Annie waited for him.

"How are you, Annie?" he asked.

"I'm getting worse, Jonah. I'm more dependent on the laudanum than I've ever been."

"That's normal. The longer you take the drug, the more you need. It affects your mind, your body, your thoughts, and your movements. Eventually, you can't even function without it."

Annie squeezed her eyes shut. She couldn't allow herself to get to that point.

"When do you want to start, Annie?" he asked.

"We might as well start now. There's no sense in waiting."

"That's a wise decision," Jonah said, reaching for Annie's hand and holding it for a second. "Don't worry. You'll be fine. Jack will be with you. So will I."

She looked at Jack, and he smiled at her.

"May I go to see Lillie before we begin?" she said.

"Yes. Jonah and I will get a room ready for you," Jack said.

Annie rose and walked to the door.

"Just be sure Mrs. Crawford is there, Annie," Jonah said before she left the room.

"I will."

She left the room and went to see Lillie. The baby was awake, and Mrs. Crawford and Molly were playing with her. Cook had sent up a plate of biscuits, and Molly was breaking one into small pieces and giving them to Lillie one at a time.

Annie spent as long as she dared with her daughter, but eventually had to tell her goodbye.

She walked down the hall on legs that trembled beneath her. She was thankful that Jack had chosen a room on the other side of the mansion, so no one could see or hear her.

She opened the door and entered the room.

The room was sparsely furnished, with nothing in it but a bed, a bedside table, and two cushioned chairs. Annie thought how bleak her surroundings would be for the next few days.

"Are you ready to begin, Annie?"

She tried to smile. "Would you let me wait if I said I wasn't?"

Jonah returned her smile. "No, probably not. I would simply tell you that putting the treatment off wouldn't make it go away, and would only make it more difficult."

"That's what I thought," she said. "So we might as well begin." She sat on the edge of the bed.

"Why don't you sit down with your wife, Jack? She'll be fine for a while."

Jack sat down beside her and reached for her hand.

"What's going to happen now, Jonah?" she asked.

"I'll let you and Jack sit here while I go out and get some breakfast. I'll be back in a little while. By that time, you should be starting to miss the laudanum. You've gone without it several times and are familiar with that feeling. When you experience that craving, you know you'll want more of your medicine. Except this time, you won't get it. You can have some wine, though. That will help."

He rose and poured her a glass of wine. Annie drank it. It did help, but not as much as it would if it had some laudanum in it.

She handed the glass to Jack, and he held it in one hand while he wrapped his other arm around her shoulders and brought her close to him.

"I won't go into what happens after that," Jonah said, "because that will be the hardest part."

"How long will that last?" she asked.

"There's no telling. Everyone is different. You'll fight us until the poison is all out of your system. Then you'll sleep."

She nodded. She wasn't looking forward to the next few days, but she would endure whatever happened. She couldn't let the poison control her like it did. For her daughter and her husband, she wouldn't.

"When I return, I'll bring Molly with me. She'll be here to help."

Annie smiled. "I'm glad."

"Very well," Jonah said. "I'm going to get something to eat. I'll be back shortly."

She watched Jonah leave the room then leaned into Jack and buried her head beneath his chin. His heart pounded beneath her ear, and his breathing became heavy.

"Don't worry about me, Jack. I'll be fine."

"I know you will, sweetheart. I don't doubt it one bit."

"I wish I had never taken that first glass of laudanum," she said. The craving was getting stronger and stronger. Her body trembled, and Jack tightened his grasp.

"You didn't take that first glass of laudanum, sweetheart. You were given that first glass. Forcefully. And you have Colin to blame for what happened to you."

"Yes," she agreed.

"If the choice had been yours to make, you wouldn't be dependent on laudanum right now."

Annie took a trembling breath. "I wish I could turn back the hands of time," she said. She hoped Jack could understand her. Her teeth chattered so hard that she was afraid he couldn't.

"So do I," he said, then leaned down and kissed her forehead, then her cheek. "I would never have left you."

"Yes, you would have. That was what you did."

"I imagine you're right. That's what I did. But it won't be any longer. From now on, I don't ever intend to leave your side."

"I love you," Annie whispered. She needed Jack to know that. It was important.

"And I love you, sweetheart," he replied.

They held each other until Jonah returned. A short while later, Molly joined them.

Annie was glad. Her nerves were taking over her body, and she knew it wouldn't be long before she lost control.

She drank more of her wine, then handed her glass to Jack. Her body trembled, and she found herself lying on the bed. Her husband sat on one side of her, and Molly on the other. The girl rinsed a cloth in a basin of water and wiped the perspiration from Annie's face.

She tried to remain lucid, but she went in and out of consciousness as her mind floated from one realm to another.

A short time later, someone in the room released a bloodcurdling scream, and Annie realized it was her.

JACK SAT AT Annie's bedside and held her hand. Her grip was intense, the pain she was suffering extreme.

"How much longer?" he asked Jonah. Jack had stayed with her much of the morning and afternoon, but when it got too intense, he would leave her for short intervals to walk the halls.

"Prepare yourself, Jack. It will get worse."

A knot clenched in his gut. *Worse?* How could it get worse? Her cries were the most gut-wrenching sounds he'd ever heard. The pain she was suffering was almost more than he could bear watching.

"She didn't get this way overnight—she won't get rid of the poison overnight," Jonah added.

Jack watched as she thrashed on the bed. He took a fresh cloth when Molly handed him one and wiped the perspiration from her face and neck and arms.

"Molly, get your mistress another night rail. This one is soaked through."

The servant left the room, and he held Annie down. Her thrashing became more violent.

"Be careful, Jack," Jonah warned. "She's battling a multitude of monsters that are fighting to get out of her."

Jack heard the warning, but he was more worried that Annie might hurt herself than he was that she would do *him* harm.

"No!" she screamed as she fought. "They're here! They're going to kill her! Oh, my baby! My baby! Give her back! You can't take her!"

He listened to the terror in her voice and knew what she was fighting against. She was battling the men who'd come to take Lillie from her. Her baby was being ripped from her arms a second time.

"No!" Annie yelled again, and swung out her arms. Her fist connected with Jack's shoulder with such force that it knocked him off balance.

Jonah rushed over and caught Annie as she leapt from the bed. From behind, he wrapped his arms around her waist and held her as she flailed violently.

Jack wanted to help her, but there was nothing he could do. She was at war with forces that were battling to dominate and destroy her.

"No! No! No!" she continued as she struggled with the enemy that consumed her.

"Pour her a glass of wine," Jonah ordered, and Jack filled a glass and held it to Annie's mouth. She drank it as if she were dying of thirst. "That's enough," Jonah said, and Jack held the glass out of her reach. "Set the glass on the table. We'll give her more in a little while."

He followed Jonah's instructions, then watched her fight the doctor for as long as he could. When her suffering became too much for Jack to endure, he ran from the room. He couldn't bear to see the love of his life suffer any more.

❧

CHAPTER FIFTEEN

HOUR AFTER HOUR, Annie screamed and fought the evil forces that attacked her. She struggled against the hostile devils that had a hold on her and refused to release her.

One day turned into another, and still she battled her demons.

Jack raked his fingers through his hair. "If I could get my hands on Colin Graves right now, I'd gouge his eyes out and make him suffer like Annie is suffering."

"He's not the only one bringing opium into the country," Jonah said. "There are fortunes to be made in the sale of opium, and even our government doesn't realize what a danger it is. Until they do, every man and woman in England will be able to walk up to any market stall and purchase a bottle of laudanum for mere pennies."

"Why do they allow it?"

"Did you give it a thought before it happened to your own wife?"

Jack felt the shameful truth of what Jonah had just said. He'd been content to ignore the problem until it reared his ugly head in his own life. Most of the country's population went about their business just as he had, in exactly the same ignorant way.

Jonah held Annie as she struggled. "Annie's just one of thousands."

Jack stepped over to them and reached out. "Let me hold her for a while," he said, taking Annie from Jonah's arms.

"If she calms any, lay her down on the bed."

But she didn't calm. Her rants and screams and fighting continued, even when the doctor held cups of liquid to her mouth.

"She needs to consume as much liquid as we can get down her. Molly," Jonah said, "get your mistress some dry clothes and bring up a pitcher of cool water and another bottle of wine."

The young girl left the room and returned with the items Jonah had requested. He poured some of the cool water in a cup and held it to Annie's mouth. She drank it as if she were dying of thirst.

For hours, Jack held her while she thrashed in his arms. Eventually, her struggles lessened. Whether that was because the poison was leaving her body or because she was wearing down from the fierceness of her fighting, he didn't know. But he experienced his first glimmer of hope. Perhaps her battle was coming to an end. Perhaps the opium was leaving her body.

Jack rose with Annie in his arms and placed her on the bed, then stripped her of her wet clothes and ordered a bath be brought up.

When he'd bathed her and washed her hair, he dressed her in the clothes Molly brought. Then he placed her in the bed and covered her with fresh sheets.

"Thank you, Molly. Your mistress and I owe you a great deal," he said. "You've watched over her long enough. Go down and get something to eat from Cook, then go and rest. I'll watch over her now."

"Yes, Major. Is it over, do you think?" Molly asked.

"Yes. It will soon be over."

She nodded and, with tears glimmering in her eyes, left the room.

Jack returned to Annie's side. She'd collapsed as if she'd lost consciousness and slept as if her body could not struggle any longer.

"She'll sleep now," Jonah verified.

"How long?"

"A day or two, if not longer."

"And then it's over?"

"The hardest part, yes."

"What's next?"

"The rest of her life. Learning to live without laudanum."

ANNIE SLOWLY OPENED her eyes and looked around the room. Jack slept in the chair beside her bed, and Jonah sat in the chair on the other side of the room.

"Are you finally waking?" Jonah asked when she took a deep breath.

"How long have I been asleep?"

"A little over a day," he answered. "How do you feel?"

"Like I'm in a foggy dream," she said.

"That's normal."

Jack jerked out of his sleep and smiled at her. "Good morning, sleepyhead. Welcome back to the living."

"Was I terrible?" Annie asked.

"To us?"

"Yes. I'm sorry if I was."

"It was a walk in the park for us," Jack answered. "I don't think it was for you, though."

"What was it like for me?"

Jack and Jonah shared a look, then her husband turned back to her. "I think I would describe your journey as a…walk through hell and back. Am I close, Jonah?"

"Yes. You're close. How much do you remember?"

She shook her head. "Nothing. I don't remember anything past the pain when it first started. I needed the medicine. I was desperate for it."

The doctor nodded. "That's usually the way it goes."

"What day is today?" Annie asked.

"Thursday," Jonah answered.

"It took me five days to get rid of the poison in me?"

Jack squeezed her hand. "Don't, Annie," he said when tears filled her eyes. "It's over now."

"I hate Colin more now than I did before, and my hatred for him before was immense."

"I feel the same," he admitted. "I didn't think I could hate anyone so much until I watched what you had to go through."

"Where's Lillie?" she asked.

"Molly has her. She's been helping you, then she went to the nursery and took care of Lillie." Jack stood. "Would you like to see her?"

"Yes."

Annie was so anxious to see Lillie that she could barely contain herself. She would finally see her baby with clear vision instead of a foggy haze. She would finally be able to hold her daughter and remember every detail of her visit, what she said to her daughter, and how Lillie reacted.

Jack went to the door and called for a servant to bring Molly and Lillie to the bedroom.

"Would you help me up?" Annie asked when he returned.

"Of course."

He helped her sit on the edge of the bed, then assisted her when she stood to put on a robe. When she was presentable, Jack led her to a cushioned chair. The moment she was settled, the door opened and Molly entered with Lillie in her hands.

"Hello, baby girl," Annie said, reaching out to gather her daughter and put her on her lap. "Oh, I've missed you," she said, kissing her daughter on the cheek, then hugging her. "Have you been a good girl for Molly?" Annie asked with tears in her eyes.

"She's been a very good girl," Molly said. "She's becoming quite the runner."

"Oh, my big girl," Annie said, then let Lillie squirm off her lap. The minute her feet hit the floor, she took off at a run toward Jack. "I see she wants her papa," Annie said when Jack picked the child up in his arms and swung her around. It was the most precious sight Annie had ever seen, and the image of her husband and her daughter playing would stay with her for the rest of her life.

Thanks to Jonah and Jack, there wouldn't be any more forgotten memories.

"How do you feel?" the doctor asked when Molly took Lillie back to her room and she was alone with Jack and Jonah.

"I feel good," Annie said with a smile.

"Now," he said, "how do you *really* feel?"

"I feel…good," she answered. "I really do, but…I wouldn't say no to a glass of wine with laudanum in it if you offered it to me."

"Which you know I'm not going to do," Jonah replied.

"How long will this last?" she asked. "This need?"

Jonah rose and poured a small amount of wine in a glass. "Wine, with no laudanum," he said, handing it to her.

She took a small sip.

"As to how long the craving for the drug will last, it will last forever, Annie."

She closed her eyes in an effort to block out what Jonah had just said.

"That's the worst part," he said.

"What's the best part?" Jack asked, reaching for Annie's hand and holding it.

"The best part is that the desire for the drug will become less and less. Eventually, a day will pass when you don't even think about wanting any. Then two days, and three. Until finally you won't think of it at all."

Annie looked from Jonah to Jack. "I can't wait for that day to come," she said with tears in her eyes.

THE NEXT FEW weeks contained a rush of enchanting memories. She and Jack grew closer than they'd ever been. Lillie went from walking and running to investigating anything she could reach. It took all of Annie and Molly's quickness to stop the child from getting into things she had no business getting into.

Jack took Annie around the estate, stopping to visit at a different tenant's cottage every day. He wanted her to meet all their tenants. Annie took a basket of baked goods and canned goods as a welcome gesture. She found she really enjoyed the tenants and couldn't wait to plan a picnic with everyone in attendance, including Quinn and Theo and their families, and all the tenants and their children. She'd make sure even the staff could come. It would be a grand affair.

But most important, Annie had an idea she'd been mulling over for several weeks. Actually, she'd been considering it since she woke up after ridding herself of the terrible poison that had taken over her body. And her mind. But first she wanted to discuss her idea with Jonah as soon as he returned from Whitstable.

Several days after she was rid of the drug, the doctor had informed them he had to return to Whitstable. He had patients to see to. But he promised that he would return in four weeks.

Those four weeks were up, and he'd sent word that he would arrive in time for dinner that evening.

Annie planned a special dinner—partly to thank Jonah for everything he'd done for her, and partly to feed him a hearty meal, since he rarely ate well. That was a drawback of living alone and not knowing how to cook.

She went to the window and watched for their guests to arrive.

"Are you watching for Jonah, sweetheart? Should I be jealous?"

Annie laughed, then stepped into her husband's arms and wrapped her arms around his neck. She stood on her tiptoes and kissed him with all the love she felt for him. She wanted to erase any thought he might have that she thought of anyone other than him.

He answered her kiss with one that matched her passion, then kissed her again before lifting his head. "Very well, my little hoyden. I'm convinced."

"Convinced of what, love? That I'm so consumed with love for you that I don't have a corner of my heart to squeeze anyone else into?"

"Yes," he said, then kissed her again.

"There was never anyone but you, Jack, and there never will be. You are the only man I will ever love."

"Oh, I wish I could say that you were the only woman I will ever love," he said, touching his forehead to hers. "But alas, there is another who has stolen my heart."

She took a step back. "And who might that be, husband?"

"She's the fairest lass I've ever seen, with golden hair and midnight-blue eyes, and the merriest laugh I've ever heard."

"Does this lass dance as well as I do?" Annie teased.

"Alas, no. She has no skill on the dance floor yet."

"And does she carry on mesmerizing conversations that enthrall you with her wit and humor?"

"Alas, no. Her conversations lack substance. But she is quite humorous."

"Well, that is one point in her favor," Annie said, leaning back into Jack's arms.

"Yes, so perhaps I would be wise in staying with the lass I have and not look for another."

She wrapped her arms around his neck again and kissed him. "That would be a wise decision. You know, the day will come when she will find someone younger and more to her liking, and she will toss you aside because you have got too old."

"Do you think so?"

"Younger women are always fickle in that regard. You should probably stay with the woman you have in your arms at the moment. I'm sure she will be more than enough for you to handle."

Jack kissed her on the forehead. "I think you are correct. She has already proven herself to be as much as I can handle."

She kissed her husband a final time before there were voices in the foyer and their butler announced Jonah's arrival.

"Come in," Jack called as both of them turned toward the door.

"Had you given up on me?" Jonah asked, walking in.

"Not at all," Annie said. "I knew you would be here."

Jack poured them each a drink, and Annie led Jonah to a chair.

"How are you doing, Annie?" the doctor asked.

"I am doing fine. There were some rough days at the beginning, and even now there is one every once in a while, but I find something to occupy my time and forget about my cravings."

"Good for you. Keeping busy is the best way to forget about the poison that was destroying your body."

"Hopefully, every day will get better, and when I look back on this time of my life, I won't even remember what it was like."

"That's what I wish for you, too," Jonah said.

Just then, the door opened and dinner was announced. They all went in to the dining room and enjoyed a wonderful meal. When it was over, Annie led Jack and Jonah to the drawing room for a drink.

"Very well, Annie," Jack said after they'd visited for a few minutes. "Out with it. I know you have something on your mind. You've been planning something for days now. Let's hear it."

She looked at her husband. "How do you know that?"

"Husbands have a way of knowing such things about their wives. Just remember that when you think to hide secrets from me."

They all laughed, then Annie looked at the doctor. "I would

like to open a hospital. And I'd like you to run it, Jonah."

⊱⊰

JACK LOOKED AT his wife, expecting to see her laugh, because he and Jonah were taking her seriously when her comment was obviously a joke. A very funny, impossible joke.

But she wasn't laughing. In fact, the expression on her face was gravely serious.

"Please explain yourself, Annie," Jack said, struggling to keep an open mind and not squash Annie's idea before she even had a chance to explain it.

"Do you remember when we toured the estate last week?" she asked.

"Yes."

"In the northeast corner of Burnhaven Estate is a—"

"A former convent that has been abandoned," he finished for her.

"Yes, an abandoned convent, in quite acceptable condition. It's not huge, but it has two wings, separated by a spacious garden area. It just has twelve rooms—six in each wing, and a large dining hall flanked by two smaller sitting rooms."

Jack sat forward in his chair, intrigued. "Are you considering converting this abandoned convent into the hospital, Annie?"

"Yes," she admitted.

"What kind of hospital?"

"A place where people with a dependence on laudanum or opium can get the treatment I received."

Jack turned to Jonah to see his reaction and was amazed at the positive expression on the doctor's face.

"What do you think, Jonah? Is this something you think would be beneficial?"

Jonah smiled. "I definitely think it would be beneficial. I also think it is the most remarkable idea I've ever heard. But how are you going to fund your hospital?"

"It's not my hospital, Jonah," she said. "It will be yours. You will be in charge of overseeing it completely. You'll hire any staff you need. And we'll fund it by charging a fee. Each patient will pay a certain amount. It will cover the cost of housing, the medical staff, and everything else we need."

"But not every patient will be able to pay full price for their treatment," Jack interjected.

"I've considered that. We will advertise for patrons who are willing to pay for the patients that cannot pay the full amount. And in time we will accrue a profit that we can put back into the hospital. That is, of course, after all monthly expenses have been paid and Jonah has received wages."

"What do you think, Jonah?" Jack asked.

"I think this just might work," the doctor said excitedly. "And we can grow much of our own food. The patients can help with this. We'll have to have something to keep them occupied after they've gone through treatment, so we'll have plots of land to turn into a garden."

"And we can keep a few cattle for milk," Annie said, "and chickens for eggs, and cows and pigs and sheep. Maybe we can even sell wool to add to our income."

"And the nuns had several fruit trees on the property," Jack added. "I've never paid much attention to what kind of trees they are, but I know there are several apple trees."

"Oh my," Jonah said. "You've really considered several of the problems we're going to encounter, but who are we going to target for our patient list? Men? Or women?"

"Both," Annie said.

"Both?" Jack said. "How are you going to manage that?"

"Quite simply. One wing will be used to house female patients, the other for the male patients. We'll put a wall between the two wings to separate them and place locked doors at each entrance."

Jack looked at Jonah and saw the wheels turning in the physician's mind. "What do you think, Jonah?"

"There is nothing I would like to do more with my life than work with patients who suffer from opium dependence. There is such a need for that. But first I would like to tour this convent to see if it can be adapted to a sanatorium."

"That will be on our agenda for tomorrow, then," Jack said. "We will tour our new hospital first thing in the morning."

Enthusiasm was growing inside him at the thought of providing such a worthwhile endeavor. He didn't doubt that there was a need for such an establishment. Nor did he doubt that a place where people could go to rid their bodies of the poison connected with opium would be in demand. He was just so proud of Annie for thinking to start such a place.

"I don't doubt that you are going to be pleased with the convent, Jonah. But what are you going to call it?" Annie asked.

A frown deepened across Jonah's brow. "I don't know. I haven't thought of that."

"I think it should have your name in it," she said. "It will be your hospital."

"But I don't want it to be a hospital," Jonah said. "Nor do I want my name above the door. I want its name to represent something positive."

"How about Hope's House?" Jack said.

"Yes!" Annie and Jonah said at the same time.

"Hope's House. That's perfect!" she added.

"To Hope's House," Jack said, lifting his glass to offer a toast.

"To Hope's House," Annie and Jonah repeated.

And thus was the beginning of a hospital to cure countless people with a dependence on opium.

CHAPTER SIXTEEN

ANNIE ROSE EARLY the next morning. She was excited to take Jonah to see Hope's House and find out what he thought of it. She didn't doubt that he would think it was perfect, just as she did. She didn't doubt that he would be as excited to get his hospital up and running as she was.

"Are you ready to tour your new house?" she said when she entered the breakfast room to find Jack and Jonah already eating their breakfast.

"Yes," the doctor said. "I can't wait."

Annie walked to the breakfast dishes and filled her plate with coddled eggs, sausage, some bacon, and toasted bread. "I have one thing to say," she said when she brought her food back to the table and sat beside Jack. "We're going to have to make sure you have a healthy supply of food for your patients. I can't believe how hungry I am now compared to how little I ate before. Even my loosest gowns are starting to get snug."

"That is one of the effects of not taking opium," Jonah said.

"Well, I'm going to have to cut back on Cook's pastries."

"Don't expect me to follow your example, wife," Jack said. "I enjoy Cook's pastries far too much to give them up."

"Then you can have my share," she said. "But when you start gaining weight, I'm going to order Cook to stop providing so many sweets."

"That's a cruel threat, wife."

"Well, if I have to give up sweets, it's only fair that you do too."

They all laughed at Annie's threat, then continued eating their breakfast. When they were finished, they collected their cloaks and walked out the front door.

Jack had a carriage waiting to take them to the convent. They stepped into it and moved into the lane.

The day was perfect for the drive to the convent, and Jonah asked more questions about the convent and any repairs Jack thought would have to be made.

Jack assured Jonah that the convent was in relatively good shape, other than needing a fresh coat of paint on the walls. Another attractive aspect of the convent was that every room already had a bed and a bedside table, and a small dresser for a patient's clothes.

There was nothing fancy about the rooms, but Annie assured Jonah that a rug on the floor and a vase of flowers would liven up the rooms and make them more habitable. Besides, she barely recalled what the room she herself had been in was like. And when she was well enough to remember, she was desperate to leave her room and go for walks, or visit with Jack to occupy her mind and forget about wanting the drug. There was no doubt that the patients would feel the same.

Their carriage pulled up in front of the convent, and Jonah was the first to disembark. While Jack helped Annie to the ground, Jonah stepped back and looked at the outside of the convent.

"So, what do you think?" Jack asked.

"I'm impressed," Jonah answered. "The building is in relatively good shape, and the design is perfect for a hospital with two wings."

"Let's go in and see what you think," Annie said, and hooked her arm through the doctor's as she led him to the front door.

They had to wait for Jack to unlock it, then they entered the building.

"Oh," Jonah said, looking up to the second floor. "Perfect. It's perfect."

Without waiting, he climbed the staircase on the right. He went down the hall, opening one door after another. "The rooms are perfect," he called back to Annie and Jack, who were following him at a slower pace.

"I knew you would approve of them," she said. "I knew this would make a perfect house, or hospital, or whatever we decided to call it, the first time I saw it."

"We'll call it a house. Hope's House."

"House it is," Annie said. She was unable to keep the grin from her face.

"I want to see the other wing," Jonah said, then went down the corridor. He followed the same routine with this wing as he had the other, going from room to room, opening each door and looking inside. "Perfect!" he said excitedly. "There's very little that needs to be done." He turned to Annie. "Is there a kitchen?"

"Yes, there's a kitchen. Even the nuns needed to eat."

"Of course they did," Jonah said on a laugh. "Where is it?"

"Follow me," Jack said, and led the way down the stairs and to the other side of the foyer.

"Wonderful," Jonah said when they entered the kitchen. Everything had been taken care of, from the stove, to the ovens, to the hearth, to the sinks and the counters.

"Can you see your cooks preparing meals, Jonah?" Annie asked.

"I can. I can almost smell the bread baking in the ovens."

Annie and Jack laughed, then continued on their way through the convent.

There wasn't one room Jonah was disappointed in, or thought they would have to do a great deal to in order to get it ready to take in their first patient.

Next, they went outside. They toured the gardens in the back and the plots of land that the nuns used to grow herbs and vegetables, then they walked through the orchard. They even picked some pears and apples from the trees.

"I knew you would be pleased," Annie said when they rounded the corner of the convent to come back to the front, walking toward the carriage to return to Burnhaven.

"More than you will ever know," the doctor replied. "I've dreamed of having my own hospital, and you and Jack have made it possible."

"All that's left now is to make a list of everything that has to be done in order to get Hope's House ready to open," she said. "There will be workers to hire, as well as cooks, and nurses, and—"

Annie's sentence was cut short by the sound of a loud pop.

"Get down!" Jack pulled Annie around the back of the carriage, then pushed her to the ground. "Are you all right, Jonah?" Jack yelled when he'd pulled his gun from his jacket.

"Yes! Was that a gunshot?"

"Take care of Annie!" Jack called out, then ran toward the shooter.

"Jack! No!"

JACK CHASTISED HIMSELF. He should have been watching more closely. He should have known that Colin Graves would be watching for them to be careless and step out into the open.

And now they'd created the perfect opportunity for him.

Thankfully, there were several trees and an outbuilding or two that Jack could use for protection as he made his way to where he thought Graves was hiding.

He knew this was a fight to the death. Graves had no intention of giving up. He didn't want to just scare Jack. He wanted to kill him. Then he intended to kill Annie.

Jack had separated himself from Annie and Jonah to keep her

out of Graves' line of fire. He had to do whatever he could to make sure the smuggler didn't survive.

Another shot rang out and hit the tree that Jack was hiding behind. Graves obviously knew where he was, as he fired again, this time striking right above Jack's head.

"You're a dead man, Washburn. I have no intention of letting you leave alive."

"And I have no intention of letting you kill me," Jack replied.

Graves laughed, a demented sound, as if his anger at losing riches from the opium he'd smuggled and his intense hatred for Jack had pushed him over the edge of sanity.

Jack studied his surroundings and made a dash for the next closest tree. If he could manage to get there, Graves would be exposed and Jack would have a clear shot.

He waited until Graves took aim and fired again, then he ran.

Graves fired a second shot, and Jack felt a fiery sting along his ribs. He was hit, but it wasn't so bad that it would stop him. Only slow him down a bit.

He dove for protection behind an overgrown hedge and waited for Graves to move. Jack couldn't remain where he was. There was no advantage to his position. He would be forced to come out, and when he did—

"Colin!" Annie yelled from behind the carriage. "Give up."

"Get back, Annie," Jack yelled.

"No, Jack. I want to see Colin's face when I put a bullet through his heart."

Graves laughed again, as if her words were a hilarious joke. As if he didn't expect the opium-addled Annie to make such preposterous threats and mean them. He didn't take her seriously at all.

"Come out, Colin," she said.

"Annie! Stay down!" Jack yelled.

He was terrified. What did she think she was doing?

And then she did the unthinkable. She stepped out from behind the carriage and stood in the open. She was a perfect target for Graves to aim at. To hit. To kill.

"Annie! Get back!"

"No, Jack. Colin won't kill me—will you, Colin?"

"I will, Annie!" Graves shouted.

"No, you won't. You could have killed me a dozen times in all the months you held me captive, and you didn't. Why was that? I want to know why you didn't kill me when you had the chance. Why, Colin?"

"Don't you know, Annie?"

"No. You tell me."

Graves was silent.

"You love her, don't you, Colin," Jack growled, as if accusing the crazed man of some heinous crime.

Graves remained silent.

"Tell her!" Jack demanded.

"Yes. I love her. I love you, Annie."

A look of shock and disbelief crossed her face, and she reached out to grab the carriage in an effort to steady herself.

"I've always loved you. I've loved you from the day your father married my mother and brought us to our new home."

"Then why did you turn me into an opium fiend? Why did you force me to write that letter to Jack? Why did you take away my baby?" she screamed.

"Because he loved you, Annie," Jack said. "He thought if he made you so unlovable, I wouldn't want you any longer. He thought I couldn't love you enough to accept all your faults. But I never stopped loving you. And now he realizes the only way to force me to give you up is to kill me."

"Yes! With Jack dead, you'll be alone," Graves said. "You'll have to turn to me. I'm all you'll have left!"

"Oh, Colin," Annie said. There was a certain sadness in her voice.

Jack knew she couldn't let her stepbrother believe there was any chance that she could love him. She could never give him what he wanted.

"Jack is the only man I will ever love, Colin. He possesses my heart. Even if you kill him, I'm still his. He'll take my heart with him to the grave."

"No!" Graves cried out. "That can't be. Don't you see? I love you, Annie. I'll give you anything you want. Anything you need. I have money now."

"I don't want money, Colin. I have everything I need. I have Jack. I have Lillie."

"But I can give you more."

"How, Colin?" Jack asked. "You're a smuggler. You're wanted by the authorities. How are you going to give Annie everything she wants when you're swinging from the end of a rope?"

"That won't happen, Washburn. I may not be in charge of the operation, but the man who is has more power than you can even imagine."

"Who?"

Graves laughed again. "You aren't going to get me to reveal who he is, Jack. The fact that I'm the only one who knows his identity is what's kept me alive this long. He's my insurance. Even if you arrest me, he'll save me 'cause he knows I'll shout his name from the rafters if he doesn't."

"Doesn't it bother you that you're such a threat to him?" Jack asked. "What makes you think he'll allow you to live when one word from you could take him down?"

"Just consider it honor among thieves. That's a good term for it."

"Haven't you heard that there's no honor among thieves, Colin?"

"There is in this case. He knows I'm more than willing to watch him swing alongside me should he betray me. He knows I won't hesitate to tell the world who the mastermind behind the smuggling ring is—"

A single shot rang out and stopped his words. Graves fell to the ground.

"Get down, Annie. Get down!" Jack shouted.

Jonah grabbed her and pulled her behind the carriage.

"I got him," Commander Waterford said, stepping out into the open. "You're safe now."

Jack looked at Waterford, then at Graves, lying on the ground. Blood streamed from his body and soaked into the dirt around him.

Jack struggled to understand what had just happened. Graves wasn't supposed to die. Not until he'd revealed the name of the man he took orders from. Not until Jack knew who was truly behind the smuggling ring.

He turned to Waterford. "Why? Why did you shoot him? He was almost ready to give up."

"No, he wasn't," the commander said. "He would never have given up."

"He was volunteering valuable information!"

"He didn't know any valuable information, Major Washburn."

"He did. He would have told us the name of the—"

Before Jack finished his sentence, another loud gunshot rang out and Waterford dropped to his knees.

Jonah rushed to see if there was anything he could do to help Waterford, but Jack knew there was nothing. The commander was wounded too badly. He was going to die.

The doctor locked his gaze with Jack's and shook his head.

"Why?" Jack asked, kneeling on the ground beside Waterford. "Why did you do it?"

"What?" Waterford asked through ragged breaths. "Smuggle?"

"Yes."

"For the…money. Why…else? I just wanted…enough to…finally…enjoy…li—" Waterford whispered with his final breath.

Jack turned to stare at Graves, who still held the gun he'd used to kill Waterford. Jack kicked it out of his hand then dropped down beside him.

"Traitor," Colin whispered through the blood in his mouth.

"Who? Waterford? Was he your leader?"

"Traitor—" he said, then breathed his last.

Jack lifted his gaze and stared at Annie and Jonah.

"Was this man the commander of the smuggling operation?" Jonah asked, pointing at Waterford.

Jack nodded, then placed his arm around Annie's shoulders. She knelt close to Graves. Tears filled her eyes and spilled down her cheeks.

"How could he have done what he did to me? If he loved me like he claimed, how could he have given me opium and taken Lillie away from me and given her to his mother? What kind of man would do that?"

"The kind of man who has never been shown any love. The kind of man who didn't know how to give of himself, but only how to take by force."

"Oh, Jack," she whispered. "How sad. What a waste."

"Yes, Annie. What a waste."

Jonah took care of Jack's bullet wound, then the three of them climbed into the carriage and returned to Burnhaven.

When they arrived home, Jack sent some men to get Commander Waterford and Colin Graves and take them to London. While they were gone, Jack wrote a letter to the acting commander explaining what had happened, and promised that he'd come to London at his earliest convenience and tie up all the loose ends.

Then Jonah made him lie down to rest until Cook had lunch ready. Jack was more than happy to follow the doctor's orders, at least for a little while.

Several hours later, dinner was ready, and Jack joined Annie and Jonah.

"You never had a chance to tell us what you thought of the convent," Jack said to Jonah while they were eating. "Do you think it will work as your hospital?"

"I think it's perfect. Other than a layer of paint in the rooms, there's little else that has to be done."

Jack looked at Annie and smiled. "Your hospital is going to become a reality, Annie. You're going to help a lot of people."

Her eyes filled with tears. "I couldn't ask for anything more."

"Neither could I," Jonah said, lifting his glass in a toast.

Annie and Jack followed his lead and toasted to the success of Hope's House.

"Do you know how many people you're going to help with this?" Jack asked.

"Hundreds, I hope," Jonah answered.

"And in time, hopefully the government will realize what a problem opium is to the people of England," Annie said.

"I'm not sure how soon that will be," Jonah said. "Especially since our queen has a special liking for the drug herself."

Her eyes opened wide.

"Are you sure?" Jack asked, not wanting to believe Jonah's revelation.

"I wish I weren't," the doctor answered, then finished his dessert.

Chapter Seventeen

ANNIE WALKED THROUGH the crowds of people gathered to enjoy their end-of-harvest picnic. The townspeople had been invited, along with the Burnhaven tenants and their families. Quinn and Cassie and their family were there, and Theo and Livie and their family.

Even Jonah had taken a day off from working at Hope's House to enjoy the festivities.

Several of the townspeople showed such interest in Hope's House that he spent the day taking wagonloads of people to tour through the hospital. He came back after each trip beaming from ear to ear. Not only had he received glowing praise from everyone who saw the progress he'd made on the old convent, but he even had several people who were interested in working there.

Finally, the sun lowered in the sky, and after everyone had finished eating, a few of the guests took out their musical instruments and played some rousing tunes. Several couples took the opportunity to dance to the songs, and before long, nearly everyone was joining in.

"This was a wonderful idea, Jack," Annie said when her husband came to stand beside her. "Everyone is having a marvelous time."

"Including you?" he asked.

"Especially me. Do you know what today is?"

Jack looked at her with a frown on his face. "Is it your birthday? Did I miss it?"

"No. It's not my birthday. Something better than my birthday."

"Well, it's not my birthday. And it's not Lillie's birthday."

"No," she said, shaking her head. "It's been six months since the day I gave up my medicine."

Jack smiled a grin that lit his whole face, then lowered his head and pressed his lips to hers. "Do you know how proud I am of you?"

"Yes, I do. You tell me often enough."

"You are one of the bravest people I know. What you have managed proves that you are the most remarkable woman I've ever met."

"When Jonah gets his house open, there are going to be many more remarkable men and women who conquer that awful drug."

"Yes, there are," he said, then kissed her again.

"Is such a display allowed in public?" Theo said, coming up beside them with his wife. Quinn and his wife were with them.

"Tonight is a perfect night for such a display," Jack said. "Annie just told me some fantastic news."

"What?" they chorused.

Annie was reluctant to reveal that opium used to be something she took regularly. Her dependency on the poison was something she wanted to keep buried in her past, where it belonged.

"I was about to tell Jack that he was going to be a father again."

"What?" he exclaimed. "Are you sure?"

"Yes, I'm sure."

"Congratulations, Annie," both Livie and Cassie said while their husbands patted Jack on the back.

Annie had grown extremely fond of Livie and Cassie since

they'd come several days ago, and had invited the two couples to spend the following week at Burnhaven to get to know them even better. Livie and Cassie were exceptional women. Cassie spent her days and nights caring for their five children, as well as taking care of the estate books for her husband. Livie ran the Angel's Wings Orphanage and Foundling Home yet still found time to organize the making of enough jams and jellies to stock their shop in London, which provided the money they needed to run the orphanage.

Both women were extremely interested in Hope's House. In fact, tomorrow they were all going to tour the place and see the progress Jonah had made on getting it ready to open.

Word had spread rapidly about its purpose, and Jonah already had several patients on a list to begin treatments. Annie didn't doubt for one second that the day would come when they would have more patients than they could handle.

"People are beginning to leave," Jack whispered to her. "We might circle the grounds and tell our guests goodnight."

"Yes," Annie agreed, taking her husband's arm and walking with him to thank their guests for coming.

When all the guests were gone, Quinn, Theo, Jack, and their wives retired to the house and sat together in the drawing room.

"This was a fantastic day," Quinn announced, lifting his glass to make a toast.

"Yes it was," Theo said, joining him. "You are to be complimented, Jack. Annie. The day couldn't have gone better."

"Thank you," Jack said. "But Annie deserves most of the credit."

"Which I will gladly accept, even though the idea for the picnic was Jack's and he did most of the work setting up the tables and chairs," she said.

Everyone laughed.

"But I still can't believe that Commander Waterford was the ringleader of a gang of opium smugglers," Theo remarked. "Did you know before Graves shot him, Jack?"

"I knew someone was giving Graves orders," Jack replied. "He wasn't intelligent enough to organize an operation as large as this. But it wasn't until Graves was about to surrender and Waterford killed him to stop him from talking that I realized who it was."

"I wish we would have been there," Quinn said. "There's already talk of a commendation for you, Jack. Which you deserve."

"No," Jack said. "I didn't do anything. Colin Graves is the one who took Waterford down. I just stood by while he made the decision to shoot him."

"But you are considered a hero by the queen. I think you should consider what you would like her to gift you this time when she asks."

"All I want is to be left alone to raise my family and live my life in peace."

"That's easy enough," Quinn said. "But Waterford's position is open, you know."

"That's not anything I want," Jack replied.

"You'd make an excellent commander, Jack," Annie said.

"So would Quinn or Theo."

"I like my life the way it is," Quinn said.

"Me too," Theo chimed in.

"So we're all in agreement," Jack said, then refilled their glasses.

The three friends and their wives regaled one another for several more hours until at last they tired and went to bed.

"ARE YOU SURE you aren't interested in Waterford's position?" Annie asked Jack after they'd made love.

"I'm quite positive," he said. "I left you once before, and look what happened. I have to stay home to make up for lost time, and

I won't be able to do that if I leave you for months at a time."

"Are you sure?"

"I'm more sure of that than I've been of anything in my life. I have a home and a family and a baby on the way. Why would I leave that for a thankless position with the government?"

"You forgot that you not only have a home, a family, and a baby on the way, but you also have a wife who loves you more than anything in the world," Annie said, kissing her husband with all the passion and desire she felt for him.

"And you have a husband who loves you even more, my love. I don't want to miss one moment of the time we have with each other. I've missed enough and I don't want to miss one second more."

Annie nestled close to him and held him tight. "Neither do I, my love. Neither do I."

EPILOGUE

JACK AND ANNIE drove to Hope's House to celebrate the grand opening Jonah was hosting.

This would probably be the last journey Jack would allow her to make before their baby was born. He'd felt Annie was so close to having her baby that she shouldn't have made the trip today, but he also knew she'd have come on her own if he didn't bring her.

His driver took them as close as he could to the front door, then Jack escorted Annie inside.

Hope's House wasn't like any hospital Annie had ever seen. The interior was appealing and cheery, and she was sure Jonah had bought out every greenhouse between here and London to give each room a homey appearance. There were bouquets of flowers and potted ferns on every surface that was flat enough to hold one.

"Oh, Jonah," Annie said when he came over to them. "It's beautiful. You couldn't have made Hope's House any more welcoming. And look at this crowd."

"There are more people here than I ever imagined would come," Jonah replied. "The interest is overwhelming."

"Has anyone signed up yet?" Jack asked.

"We're nearly full. We can only handle one new patient every week, and so far we have a new patient coming every week through the end of the year."

"I don't believe it," Annie said. "I knew opium was a bigger problem than anyone realized, but I had no idea it was as widespread as this."

"Yes, even though the government encourages the sale and the use of opium because of the revenue it generates, the general public is living with the effects of the drug in their own homes, and they don't like it. When wage earners who are dependent on opium can't work, there's no money coming in, and children go hungry. The damage the drug is doing is indescribable."

"Oh, Jonah. I can't tell you how fortunate we are to have you," she said. "You'll never know how much I appreciate everything you've done for me."

"Let's hope all my patients do as well as you did," Jonah said. "Would you like a tour?"

"I would love it, but I think I need to get off my feet for a while before I do."

"Are you all right, Annie?" Jack asked.

"I'm fine. Just a little tired. That's all."

"I tried to keep her home," he groused sweetly, wrapping his arm around her waist and leading her to the nearest chair. "But you know how stubborn she can get."

"Yes," Jonah agreed. "I know exactly how stubborn your wife can get."

All of them laughed, except Annie. She clutched her stomach and gasped with pain.

"Annie?"

"Yes, Jack?"

"Are you all right?"

"No, Jack. I should have heeded your advice. I think I'd like to lie down someplace."

"Follow me," Jonah said, and led them to a private area.

Jack scooped Annie up into his arms and followed Jonah. "Are these your living quarters?" he asked, placing Annie on the bed.

"Yes," Jonah answered. "Now, if you'll excuse me for a moment, I'll go out and find someone to assist me. My nurse is somewhere in the crowd."

Jonah left the room, and Jack knelt beside Annie's bed.

"Don't worry, Jack. I'm in the best hands I could be in. We were going to send for Jonah when it was time for the babe to come anyway. I just didn't anticipate that we would come to him instead of him coming to us."

"And I'll wager Jonah didn't think his first procedure would be the birth of a baby."

"I'm sure he—" Annie released a painful cry.

"Here," Jack said. "Hold my hand. It will be all right."

She clutched his hand and held it until the wave of birthing pains eased.

The door opened, and Jonah entered the room with a middle-aged woman following him. "Annie, this is Martha. She's quite knowledgeable when it comes to birthing a babe. She was a midwife until I talked her into coming to work with me here."

"I'm glad to meet you"—Annie released another painful cry—"Martha."

Martha removed Annie's shoes and stockings, then arranged the covers. "It's a pleasure to meet you, Mrs. Washburn. Dr. Reynolds explained what my duties would entail working here, but he failed to include birthing a babe."

"An oversight, Martha," Jonah said on a laugh. "Simply an oversight. Now, Jack, why don't you leave us for a while? At least long enough for Martha and Annie to bring your baby into the world."

"I love you, Annie," Jack whispered, then gave her a kiss before he left the room.

She answered his kiss with another pain-filled cry.

JACK PACED THE halls and toured the rooms, then paced the halls some more. He was still pacing after all the guests were gone and there were only a few of the workers left to clean up.

He'd missed Lillie's birth and wasn't prepared for the long wait. One hour went by, then another, and all he heard were painful cries from Annie, then silence. He didn't know how much longer he could stay out of the room. He wanted to be with her, yet knew he wouldn't be any help at all. Only a hindrance.

Finally, he heard a heart-wrenching scream, followed by a baby's cry. Jack collapsed against the wall and braced his hands on his knees. He had a son or a daughter. He didn't know which, and he didn't care, as long as it was healthy and Annie was all right.

He paced the floor in front of the door a little while longer, then bolted upright when the door opened.

"Congratulations, Jack," Jonah said, stepping into the hall. "You have a son."

"A son? A boy?"

"Yes, a son."

"Can I go in? How is Annie? Is she all right?"

"Annie is fine. She's tired, but she's fine."

Jack stepped past Jonah and ran to Annie. She was in bed and had a little bundle in her arms.

"Have you come to meet your son, Jack?"

"Yes," he said. That was the only word he could manage.

Annie moved the blanket enough that Jack could see his son's face. He was tiny, much smaller than Jack was prepared for.

"Here," Annie offered. "Would you like to hold him?"

"Wha…what if I hurt him?"

She laughed, and so did Jonah and his nurse. "You won't hurt him. He's not that fragile. He's a Washburn."

"Oh, right," Jack said, then took the child from his wife's arms and held him. "What are we going to call him?"

"I named Lillie," Annie said. "So you can name this one."

"I'd like to call him Franklin, after my father. Is that all right?"

"That's just fine. Frank he is. Little Frankie Washburn. I like it."

"So do I," Jonah agreed. "It's a good, solid name. And I'm glad you chose to have him here. It's only appropriate that our first procedure be a birth."

"And it's only appropriate that Jonah's first patient is you, Annie," Jack said, leaning down to kiss his wife. "It was your idea that started this project, and you and our son brought it to life."

Annie lifted her gaze to meet his. "I love you, sweetheart. More than I can ever say."

"You don't have to say it, Annie. I know how much you love me. I feel the same about you."

And Jack kissed his wife with all the love he felt for her. As much as he always had and always would.

About the Author

Laura Landon taught high school for ten years before leaving the classroom to open her own ice-cream shop. As much as she loved serving up sundaes and malts from behind the counter, she closed up shop after penning her first novel. Now she spends nearly every waking minute writing, guiding her heroes and heroines to find their happily ever afters.

She is the author of more than a dozen historical novels, including SILENT REVENGE, INTIMATE DECEPTION, and her newest Montlake Romance release, INTIMATE SURREN-DER.

Her books are enjoyed by readers around the world.